NUMBERS CAN KILL

There are hordes of spiders to every human being on earth.

Fortunately, human beings have always held the upper hand over these creatures who fill us with such instinctive revulsion and primitive fear.

But suppose this balance of power changed. Suppose a new species of spider became dominant, a mutant strain that matched in strength and cunning and appetite for dominion anything that humankind possessed.

Now you don't have to suppose. You can see, if you dare. . . .

THE SPIDERS

The odds have suddenly shifted against our survival!

Big Bestsellers from SIGNET

THE
SPIDERS

by
Richard
Lewis

A SIGNET BOOK
NEW AMERICAN LIBRARY
TIMES MIRROR

PUBLISHER'S NOTE

This novel is a work of fiction. Names, characters, places, and incidents are either the product of the author's imagination or are used fictitiously, and any resemblance to actual person's living or dead, events, or locales is entirely coincidental.

COPYRIGHT © 1978 BY RICHARD LEWIS

All rights reserved. For information address The Hamlyn Publishing Group Ltd., Astronaut House, Feltham, Middlesex TW1 49AR, England.

Published by arrangement with The Hamlyn Publishing Group Ltd.

 SIGNET TRADEMARK REG. U.S. PAT. OFF. AND FOREIGN COUNTRIES REGISTERED TRADEMARK—MARCA REGISTRADA HECHO EN CHICAGO, U.S.A.

SIGNET, SIGNET CLASSICS, MENTOR, PLUME, MERIDIAN AND NAL BOOKS *are published by The New American Library, Inc.,* 1633 Broadway, New York, New York 10019

FIRST SIGNET PRINTING, JUNE, 1980

1 2 3 4 5 6 7 8 9

PRINTED IN THE UNITED STATES OF AMERICA

The
Spiders

1

Dan Mason leaned back contentedly on the Victorian rocking chair. Late autumn sunshine slanted through the leaded windows, giving the old-fashioned farmhouse kitchen a warm, cozy feel. He looked round the room, smiling as his eye followed the pitted, smoke-charred oak beams from one end of the ceiling to the other, frowning slightly as he glanced at the black iron kitchen range set into the alcove—that would have to go, he decided. The rough plastered walls, once painted white, would need another coat and Dan had a feeling that the windows, pretty though they were, would have to be replaced.

But all in all, he reckoned, the house was a good buy. There was no doubt he had made the right decision. He chuckled as he remembered the enthusiastic young real estate agent, an ambitious lad of about twenty-four, wearing a pinstripe suit and carrying a black vinyl briefcase.

"It's a cinch, Mr. Mason, a cinch," the agent had said earnestly. "Spend a little time on the house and garden, and you'll have a palace," he added, beaming. "Yes, a palace. One of the finest properties in all of Kent, this could be."

Dan certainly had plenty of time, and he had never been one to shirk tackling a job.

At sixty-seven, his two years following retirement from a managerial position in the sugar industry had not come easily to him. In his thirty-four years with the company—"Thirty-four *good* years," he maintained—Dan had made many friends, both in the factories where the sugar beet was processed and on the farms where the beet was grown.

The job had taken him through Britain, checking production at factory level as well as on the farms. Dan was never happier than when talking with farmers, instinctively understanding their problems. A favorite joke of his was that he was a "country yokel stuck in a concrete jungle," his one regret being that he had to work mostly at the head office in London.

If Dan Mason had had his way, the head office would have been a farm! His greatest joy was gardening, and although the Masons had only a small patch attached to their house in Fulham, Dan had managed to turn it into a botanical dream. All the year round it was a blaze of floral color, and his vegetables were the talk and envy of his neighbors.

A physical-fitness addict, every summer Dan played fierce tennis at his local club, and during the winter even fiercer badminton. Around the factories he was known as "Charlie Atlas," but it was his proud boast that he could take on most of the young apprentices for a few tennis sets and still not be out of breath.

Just over six foot tall, Dan's white hair, dark blue eyes, and rounded, ruddy face gave him not so much a distinguished appearance as a kindly, trustworthy look. His wife, Mary, always joked that he would make a good grandfather because he had the looks for one.

Mary was the perfect match for Dan. Unambitious and uncomplicated, she was quite content with her lot in life. In the thirty-five years they had been married there had been no traumatic tests of their relationship. She had never questioned it: Dan was her husband and that was all there was to it—nothing more. No restless feelings, no fantasies or desires. She had never known another man, never felt the need, and never allowed herself to get into situations where alternatives even had to be considered. Dan and Mary lived on a level of mellow calm—and both appreciated it.

So when the day finally came when Dan was presented with his gold watch, a canteen of stainless steel cutlery, and had his photograph taken for the house magazine, they had already decided what to do with the rest of their lives.

"It'll be nice to live out of town," Dan had said. "The thing is not to move *too* far from London. That way our friends and Alan can visit us any time they want to."

Mary agreed. As long as she could see their only son Alan she did not really care where they lived. Alan was a biologist, and although Mary could not fully understand what he did, she knew it had something to do with animals and plants. And, according to the scientific journals he brought home from time to time, he had a brilliant career marked out ahead of him.

When asked what Alan did, Mary simply said, "He lectures at the university," knowing that would stop a lot of awkward questions—questions she could not answer, due to her ignorance.

One thing she was sure of, however. She definitely approved of Alan's latest girlfriend, Louise Roberts, a laboratory technician he'd met at the university.

That could be a very timely meeting, Mary thought, what with Dan and her moving out to that lovely big house in the country. Just right for little children to run about in. . . .

The Masons had scoured the papers for weeks, looking for a suitable property within their budget. When they had come across the old farmhouse, with its one-third of an acre, they had been delighted, though Dan was surprised that the house had stood empty for a year.

"Well, you know what modern house-buyers are like, Mr. Mason," the bubbling young agent had said.

"All they're after now is a modern square box with everything in it from fitted cupboards to waste-disposal units," he claimed, shaking his head sadly. "They don't want atmosphere, a sense of traditional values. It takes a man of your years and experience to appreciate these things."

Dan had ignored the reference to his age, understanding what the young man, almost on the point of oversell, had meant.

"No, there's no doubt about it," the agent gushed on. "Dragon's Farm has got more atmosphere than a thousand modern bungalows."

"Why is it called Dragon's Farm?" Mary had asked.

"I think there used to be a hill on the land, called Dragon's Hill. There's a lot of strange legends connected with it, but as the mound was razed to the ground a couple of hundred years ago I don't think you need worry," the agent smiled.

As Dan's only objective was to get into the farmhouse as quickly as possible, he was not concerned in the least about old wives' tales or legends. With the previous owners of Dragon's Farm already away, it was just a matter of selling their own property in London and moving out. Luckily that only took a few weeks.

And here he was, happy as a schoolboy, sitting in Kent listening to the faint twilight chorus of birds. Feeling chilly, he lit a portable paraffin stove he'd brought from London and, standing with his back to it, looked down the rear garden.

There were two priorities as far as Dragon's Farm was concerned, he reckoned—central heating and putting the back garden in order. The rest of the land could wait until next spring, but autumn was ideal for digging over a vegetable plot and preparing the ground for the following year's crop.

The garden was overgrown, and what appeared to

have been a flagstone path could be seen under the long, wild grass. Weeds sprouted everywhere, and of every type—from the ground-creeping, oddly-named wild strawberry to the proud, upright thistle.

Dan sighed as he thought of the work to be done before he could even start planning the plot. But he thought it was nothing a good hard day's work couldn't conquer and with the following day being a Sunday, he could make an early start. On Monday he was returning to London to help Mary with the final packing and moving arrangements.

He made himself a light supper of corned beef and potato chips, followed by a can of ale, fixed a shelf in the kitchen, and went to bed early. He lay thinking of Mary, and how the years had slipped by with comfortable ease. He wished he could speak to her, but there was no phone at the farm. He felt cut off and isolated, and looked forward to Monday.

Dan drifted off to sleep thinking about cabbages as big as footballs, cucumbers as long as walking sticks, plums as sweet as honey, and lettuce as crisp as snow on a winter's morning, all growing in magnificent profusion in the garden he already pictured in his mind.

The following day was perfect for gardening. An invigorating freshness in the air brought a ruddy glow to Dan's cheeks as he hacked and tugged at the twisted, overgrown weeds in the back garden. He worked steadily, moving away from the house toward the old wooden fence at the foot of the plot. Behind the fence was what had once been an orchard of apple, plum, and cherry trees, but it was now a tangled mess of interlocking branches, dying trees, and broken remains of trunks.

Dan broke off for lunch about midday, pleased with his morning's work. The sky was still hard blue and the weather looked settled. No wind blew and the trees surrounding the garden were still.

As Dan leaned against the kitchen door looking out at the trees, he became aware of the stillness in the garden. It was a stillness all the more pronounced by the absolute silence. No birds chirped; no squirrels or rabbits scurried through the woods.

He knew the nearest farm was about four miles away, so he did not expect any people to wander by. But surely the normal sounds of the country should be present? He recalled the twilight chorus of the night before. That, too, had been faint, as if coming from a great distance.

Shrugging, he strolled down to the foot of the garden, stopping in front of a particularly large and wild patch of weeds in the corner of the fence. That would be his afternoon's work. A nice spot for the potato plot once the weeds were cleared.

The patch consisted mainly of wild strawberry interspersed with creepers, probably the remains of an old rose bush. The sun was almost overhead, and sweat poured off Dan's forehead. He worked with his shirt sleeves rolled up, and underneath the gardening gloves his hands felt hot and clammy.

Wiping his brow with the back of his arm, he tucked his fingers under a large spreading root and tugged. Nothing happened. He swore under his breath, but not wanting to return for the fork which he had left at the side of the house, he tried brute force once again.

This time the plant loosened, and flexing his muscles he gradually pulled the long, white, straggly root out, small heaps of dry earth falling to the side. He straightened and looked at the space left by the weed. An army of insects—black shiny beetles, wood lice, centipedes, worms, and tiny garden creatures—scurried around, frightened by the disturbance.

Dan watched them for a few minutes, until they had disappeared. "Little buggers," he thought. "Still, I suppose they keep other pests away."

A large clump of brown grass to the left of the newly made space caught his eye, and he grasped it. Pulling backward, he found it was as tough as the weed. Annoyed, and realizing he would probably have to dig up the rest of the plot, he yanked hard at the grass.

It came away suddenly, and Dan lost his balance. He fell backward and landed with a thump on his backside, still clutching the clump of coarse grass. Normally he would have laughed, but he was tired after his day's work and in no mood for humor.

He looked at the dark patch where the grass had been. He was surprised that there were no insects crawling around, but as he peered closer he noticed about a dozen holes, the sort earthworms make, but larger, spaced over the black earth.

He was about to stand up when he noticed a small movement at one of the holes. He leaned forward again and watched in amazement as a spider, its squat body almost black, emerged from the entrance carrying a squirming beetle in its jaws.

Dan had never seen anything like it before. Beside the fact that the creature looked nothing like a common garden spider—light green with long thin stalks of legs—he had never known spiders to carry their prey around with them.

The sight of this spider with its half-dead victim in its jaws made Dan shudder with disgust. He flicked it away with his gloved hand. The creature rolled to the edge of the newly uncovered earth, dropping the beetle in its fall.

Surprisingly, the creature did not scuttle away among the undergrowth, but turned—and it seemed to look directly at him, the winter sun reflecting on the hard shell of its back. Dan squatted on his knees and darted forward, pressing his thumb on top of the spider.

Through the glove he felt its back—round and solid. Puzzled, he twisted his thumb angrily, pushing the insect into the earth. He lifted his hand, expecting to see its squashed remains.

Unbelievably, the spider was still alive. Its legs were curled under its body, in ball-like defense, and it appeared to be trembling. After a few seconds, its legs shot out and it stood upright, its thick body quivering.

"Bloody thing!" Dan muttered as he brushed the spider away with the back of his hand. It landed where the wild strawberries had been, lay still for a few moments, and then slowly crawled back toward Dan.

"Jesus!" Dan laughed. "You don't give up, do you? OK, you win," he grinned. "I'll put you back with your dinner." He picked it up and put it on the back of his right hand. He looked around for the beetle but could not find it.

He gazed at the spider sitting immobile on the back of his glove. It certainly was unusual, he thought. The insect had a hard, shell-like back similar to that of a large flying beetle. Its eight legs were covered with sharp, jagged bristles, like thorns on a rosebush. Underneath its head the two biting jaws appeared unusually strong and large for its size.

Dan felt an involuntary shiver of fear run down his back as he saw the eight eyes staring unblinkingly at him. He could not explain it, but he felt as if the creature was *thinking* hate.

Dan lifted his arm to fling the spider off but, almost as if the insect realized his intention, it jumped nearly six inches, onto his uncovered arm. Dan felt a sharp prick where the spider had landed and, cursing, knocked it off to the ground.

Swearing aloud, he jumped up and crushed the spider to a pulp under the heel of his boot—not noticing the dozens of glinting eyes watching him from the other dark entrances in the earth. . . .

Dan worked until the light began to fade, and then he pottered about the house. He packed a suitcase, and laid his clothes out for the next morning, ready to catch the early train.

He shivered under a cold shower, looking forward to the day when central heating would provide an ample supply of hot water. Feeling exhausted, but not hungry, he went to bed around ten o'clock. As he spiraled into a deep, black sleep he thought about the strange silence around the farmhouse, but tiredness soon pushed that and other thoughts beyond the edge of his mind. . . .

He woke suddenly, with no trace of drowsiness. The darkness around him was almost solid. Through the open window he heard the rustling of the trees. But over that there was another sound through the blackness—a sliding, scraping, almost whispering noise.

Dan's right arm throbbed, and feeling it with his other hand he discovered it was blown up, and soft and mushy to the touch. He squeezed the pulpy flesh. He could feel nothing but the *thump-thump* of pain along his arm.

He screamed, his heart pounding wildly, and tried to sit up. Something held him back, like a thin rope across his chest. Heaving himself up, he heard a snap and then he was free. He stared ahead into the solid, enveloping darkness. The ache in his arm was forgotten for a moment as he heard the sound again. Sliding, scraping—almost whispering.

Cold ripples ran over his back, and waves of fear almost made him choke. But what was he frightened of, he wondered in a bizarre moment of lucidity. He stretched his hand through the darkness, trying to find the bedside lamp, a tall old-fashioned brass type.

His fingers found the lamp and he clutched it. Gasping with shock, he quickly pulled his hand away. Along the stalk of the lamp he had felt hard, jagged bristles, not unlike rose thorns. But the stalk was moving!

His strength almost gone, he reached out again and, trying desperately to ignore the scratching on his palm and the light tickling sensation across the back of his hand and up his arm, he found the switch and pressed it.

A circle of light flooded over the bed; the corners of the room and the window remained in shadow. Dan froze with terror, his hand still on the switch. The faded green carpet was covered with an undulating black mass which moved forward like a sea-swell . . . up and over the bed.

They stopped almost as soon as the light exposed them—trembling softly and silently. Then a few spiders began to move up Dan's left arm. The feathery touch of their legs snapped Dan into action. Raising his right hand he moved to brush the insects off. Then he screamed when he saw what had happened to his arm.

The whole arm, from the elbow down, was three times its normal size, puffed up like a huge, bruised blister. The color almost made Dan vomit. Dark blue, it was tinged with green and dark purple, and pulsed visibly, like the underbelly of a dying frog.

Hysterically, Dan tried to move out of the bed, but found himself held back. Across his chest clung the broken remains of a thick web, and around his legs the spiders had spun a crisscross pattern of silk which he found impossible to break.

His eyes widened with horror, and spittle ran from the corners of his mouth. He lay back, his mind blank and feeling only the numbing fear that had taken over his body. He looked across at the window and his mouth hung open in a silent scream.

On the window ledge a dark shape, the size of a

large crab, huddled in the shadowy gloom. Nothing in the room moved. Even the spiders on Dan's arm now stood still. Dan could not take his eyes from the black shadow at the window. He saw two indistinct tentacles rise from it, and wave slowly from side to side.

It was as if a signal had been given. The spiders began moving toward the bed—sliding, scraping, almost whispering. They crawled up the bed and over Dan, wave upon wave, pushing the front ranks forward.

He felt countless jabs in his arms and legs, in his stomach and face. His eyelids grew heavy and he tried to close them, but a sharp nipping sensation forced them open. He was aware of a blurred, jagged leg of a spider across one pupil and wanted to brush it away, but his arms were numb and useless and he found it impossible to lift them.

Just before the spiders crowded over his face, pitching him into merciful unconsciousness, he saw the black shape on the window swing from the ledge and remain suspended in the half-light for a few seconds, before gliding to the floor. . . .

When the morning sun fingered its way through the open bedroom window, casting shadows of the climbing roses on the opposite wall, there were no insects or traces of web to be seen. But an emaciated figure—with pieces of flesh hanging from its bones, and two lidless eyeballs staring at the ceiling—lay stretched on the bed in the center of the awful silence around Dragon's Farm.

2

John Murphy stared ahead in panic and frustration at the long line of stationary traffic. His stomach was knotted with tension as he tightly gripped the steering wheel of his old Humber. He was worried, more worried than he could remember ever being in his life. This time, he knew he had gone too far; he found himself in a situation that he could not control—or even cope with.

It was Monday afternoon, and he had been driving on the main trunk-road out of London toward Kent for about an hour. A thin, persistent drizzle fell, making the inside of the car steamy with condensation. A few miles ahead of Murphy's car a truck had skidded, shedding its load of timber and causing the traffic jam which he now cursed.

Angrily he wiped the windshield with the sleeve of his shirt, and then lit a cigarette, inhaling deeply. He was now smoking sixty a day, had been for the last three months, and knew he was slowly killing himself.

Shifting uncomfortably, he pulled a flat silver hip-flask from his back pocket. He gulped the whisky greedily, feeling no better for it. Cigarette ash fell on his trousers and he irritably brushed it away.

Murphy glanced at his watch and figured it would be at least two hours before he reached home—a small village in south Kent. And then he would have to confront Alison, his wife. The thought of her questioning, her inevitable sarcastic cross-examination, made him sweat. John Murphy, beneath his worry and the irritation at the traffic conditions, was a frightened man. And he knew it.

Murphy owned the only garage in his home village, and, while he was not exactly short of money, there was only so much profit a garage could make in a small village in Kent. In the twenty years he had been married to Alison he had worked hard to build up his business and an ever-widening circle of regular customers. He had also acquired the Automobile Association and Royal Automobile Club concessions for emergency calls.

Basically John Murphy was content with his lot. The house had been paid off, he and his wife took part in the social life of the village, and, not having children, they could afford to spend that bit extra on themselves. In his mid-forties he was still a good-looking man, if thinning a bit on the top, if perhaps a little untidy in his appearance and slightly grubby under the fingernails. But, as he always said, "I'm a working man, and a working man I'll be all my life." A point Alison Murphy did not like to be reminded of.

Alison, and her family, always considered that she had married below her class. Her father had been a bank manager in a nearby town, and she had been brought up to feel privileged. She met John just before he got his discharge from the army, and later, during bitter arguments, she claimed it was "the uniform I fell in love with, not the man." Fastidiously tidy, she kept their home neat at all times, never allowing a dirty ashtray to stand for more than five minutes.

Unable to have children, she hid her disappointment by involving herself in various committees and charity organizations, but could not in any way persuade her husband to join her. "It's just not my scene, love," he would tell her. "I feel uncomfortable."

Their marriage had settled down to an easy, comfortable level. For the first few years sex had been "indulged in," as Alison put it to her friend Betty, fairly regularly on Wednesday nights and Sunday mornings (by Alison's choice), but after a while any pretense soon vanished. Now they slept in separate bedrooms and Alison's only passion seemed to be the state of the house, which she redecorated every year.

John Murphy was not altogether unhappy with the situation. Alison was by no means an unattractive lady. Small, with long dark hair, she had a smooth complexion which needed no make-up. She had large, brown eyes and a small mouth. The only fault Murphy could honestly find in her was a tendency to put on weight.

But if Alison had other faults, nagged at him needlessly, worried about the cleanliness of the house, and moaned about his appearance, Murphy knew— and sometimes admitted—that he could have made a worse choice. And as far as sex was concerned, like most other people, if there was none, he was certainly not going to look hard for it elsewhere. For John Murphy liked his creature comforts too much to jeopardize them for the odd fling or two. So, all in all, until a few months ago he had felt satisfied with his lot, realizing that if he did not have a perfect love relationship, at least he had constant companionship.

But then he met Marianne Henderson. He had been called out by the A.A. to a late-night breakdown not far from the village. It was the middle of summer and the night was warm. As the lights of his Land-Rover picked out the stranded MGB sports car, he was surprised to see a young girl leaning against it, smoking a cigarette.

When he reached her he saw she was older than he initially thought, probably in her thirties. Her hair, almost black, was cut in the latest style—short and full. Her face was the type Murphy had seen only in glossy fashion magazines—perfectly made up. The shape was oval, the eyes blue and the nose small and upturned, with the mouth full and sensuous. She was wearing a plum-colored pair of slacks with sweater to match—both had an expensive look, he thought.

She smiled gratefully as he got out of the Land-Rover.

"I'm glad you're here. I almost gave up." The voice was husky, throaty, confident with breeding. An "expensive" voice.

Murphy examined the engine. The points had jammed and he easily replaced them. As always, in an effort to bring in as much money as he could, he suggested that she bring the car to the garage for a check-up the following day.

"Oh, yes," she nodded. "My husband and I have a cottage in the next village. But can't *you* come over? I'm hopeless at directions, and I'd probably get lost," she added, her eyes smiling.

Murphy looked away, for some reason feeling embarrassed.

"OK. I'll do that," he muttered, and wrote down the address she gave him.

That night he did not sleep well. He thought of Marianne, her sophistication, her sensuousness, her body. And the way she had held his hand a few seconds longer than necessary when saying good-bye. He was excited and disturbed at the same time. Excited because he thought all such feelings had died. Disturbed because he had never been in a situation like this before, and he was also terrified that something would happen and that Alison would find out.

The next day Marianne was alone. Her husband had been detained in London, she told Murphy. He pottered about the car, fiddling with carburetors, fan belt, and ignition. When the car sounded satisfactory, he asked if he could wash his hands.

In the cottage, she stood at the bathroom door watching him scrub his fingers.

"Are you married?" she asked.

He nodded.

"Happily?"

"As much as anyone can be."

"Would you like to go to bed with me?" she smiled.

He was caught offguard, but tried not to show it.

"Why not?" he laughed, aware of his heart pounding with excitement.

She led the way through to the bedroom and casually stripped in front of him. Her breasts were well-formed, though beginning to sag a little, but her body did not have an ounce of excess fat on it. Her mound was well-formed and the hair shaped in an almost perfect triangle. He stood looking at her, awkward in his own inexperience.

Smiling wistfully, and without a word, she came over to him and slowly undressed him—before pulling him down on top of her. That first time he had been nervous, too quick, and felt he had let her down.

Afterward they smoked a shared cigarette and drank some brandy. He dressed hurriedly and stood by the side of the bed as she lay stretched out, her legs slightly apart.

"Will . . . will I see you again?" he stumbled, knowing he did not want to ask the question, yet finding it impossible to stop himself.

She nodded, and taking his hand, guided it down between her legs, pressing it against the moist warmth.

"Of course, John. I *like* strong men."

He drove home slowly, trying to fight the feelings of guilt. That night he drank more than usual. Would Alison be able to guess? Could she see the difference in his attitude? Women knew these things instinctively, he had once read. Despite the thrill he experienced when he was with Marianne, he was miserable when away from home. And that had nothing to do with love.

They saw each other when she came down to the cottage; each time Murphy promising himself there would be no more. For the guilt was becoming laced with fear, and he was smoking and drinking heavily.

The week before, Marianne had asked him up to London for the weekend. At first he had refused but she managed, as always, to persuade him. Her husband was abroad. "We could have a lovely time in London," she said.

He told Alison he had to attend a car dealers' conference. Her reaction was icy.

"You've never gone before," she snapped. "Why now?"

Murphy was convinced she knew, but it was too late to back out.

He shrugged and mumbled something about the Government's new restrictions.

Alison sniffed and looked at him disdainfully.

"Well, I'm sure you won't want *me* along," she said. "You'll be wanting to stay up all night drinking and going to strip shows, I suppose."

He shrugged again and did not answer.

The weekend was a disaster, as far as he was concerned. He could not relax, imagining Alison phoning round to find out if there *was* a conference. When Sunday afternoon came, and he prepared to leave, Marianne used the oldest female tactic in the book to keep him in London. She began crying, accusing him of just using her.

He comforted her, felt her warm face against his chest, pressed her body close to him, and then, of course, they made love again.

So Sunday stretched into Monday, and he woke up feeling miserable, guilty, and frightened. This time he had definitely gone too far. They made useless love on Monday morning, and he left after lunch. Both of them knew it was over.

And here he was, stuck in the traffic, panicking at what might face him when he arrived home. He swigged the remainder of the whiskey in the flask and, annoyed that it was empty, flung it to the back of the car.

Alison Murphy glanced at the clock for about the sixth time in ten minutes. Five o'clock. Where the hell *was* John? She was not so much angry as irritated. It broke the pattern, the pattern they had established over the last twenty years.

Alison knew she had married through infatuation, and that after a few years any flush of love there had been had soon paled into insignificance. But she was proud, the bank manager's daughter. She had defied her family, gone against their wishes, but would not admit that she had been wrong. *She* would keep a fine house, feed her husband well, and give the appearance of being happily married. No one would ever be able to point the finger at her.

Not that she was unhappy, but she lived on a level of neutrality where her life with John was geared to a regular, unthinking, unquestioning structure. And that was why she was disturbed when John did not return on the Sunday, as promised. True, he had been behaving a little strangely lately, but Alison shrugged that off as being due to business worries.

Tired of sitting doing nothing, she decided to drop in on her close friend Betty, who lived in the next house.

Together they had a martini and talked about trivial matters, but Alison carefully avoided mentioning John. Even when Betty archly joked about him running off with another woman, Alison would not be drawn in. The fact was that such a thought had never even crossed her mind. It was not part of the pattern—and, anyway, married men in their mid-forties did not do such things. Not according to her code of rules.

But, once back in her own house, the thought began to take shape. Suppose he *had* met someone? Annoyed that she could even think such a thing, she told herself she was too tense and was overreacting to an innocent situation. What she needed was a bath, she thought, and went upstairs to run the water.

In the bedroom she undressed in front of a tall mirror. Naked, she looked at herself slowly. There was no doubt about it. She *was* putting on weight, but she thought she still had a good body for a woman of forty-one. Her hair remained her finest point, and if her breasts looked pale and slightly droopy that was nothing a good bra could not cure. Her thighs needed thinning, she sighed, and she gazed at the dark patch of hair at the top of them. She could have been looking at a pot of tea for all the feeling it aroused in her. Sex had lost all its magic when she discovered she could not have children. As a woman, she told herself, she was useless, although she would never admit this to John. She felt she did not have to—surely he understood.

She hung up each piece of clothing meticulously before going into the bathroom to turn off the taps. The bath was now almost full and she sank heavily into it, enjoying the water's warmth around her body. Soon she was in a half-drowsing, half-awake state, completely relaxed.

Alison, her eyes heavy, looked around the bathroom, pleased with the colors she had chosen the year before. Everything was in its place. The toothbrushes hung neatly on the rack; the tube itself had been wiped and laid above the brushes; the towels—John's and hers—were folded carefully over the heated rail. Even the spare toilet roll had a woolen cover over it.

Suddenly she sat up as she felt a cold draught at her left shoulder, coming from the half-open door. Sighing at the thought of getting out of the bath she tried to reach over to close it. As she did so she spotted something dark scuttle past the foot of the door.

Her hand still stretched out, she gazed in disbelief at the dark shadowy object now crawling silently over the carpeted floor. It was a spider! Alison hated spiders. Hated them to the point of phobia. Apart from the fact that they were dirty, she was revolted by their appearance.

Whimpering, and feeling very conscious of her nakedness, she picked up a piece of soap and hurled it at the spider. The creature stopped for a few seconds, as if startled by the soap which narrowly missed it, and then continued its menacing advance toward the bath.

"No, no, no," Alison sobbed, the breath catching in her throat.

She wanted to leap up and run from the bathroom, but the creature was between her and the door. She would feel less vulnerable with her dressing gown on, but that was hanging behind the door.

And then she saw them. A spreading pool of black creatures spilling over the top of the stairs and moving toward the bathroom. Myriad eyes glistened in the reflected light and hundreds of tiny legs moved up and down as they steadily advanced on the bath in which she lay.

Sheer icy terror gripped Alison as the first wave entered the bathroom—a mass of bristle-covered, swaying black bodies. Every childhood and adult fear she had of spiders came back to her in that instant. It was more than her mind could take—the thought that they were going to crawl over her, suffocate her with their foul bodies. Her mind-snapped and she fainted, her head slipping beneath the water, her right hand dangling over the edge of the bath.

Silently the cause of her horror climbed the side of the bath until they reached the hand. They crowded round it, crawling over each other in frenzy. Some darted over the wrist and down the arm, but stopped when they reached the level of the water.

John Murphy arrived in the village just after five, when Alison was still having drinks with Betty. Obsessed with fear and guilt, he drove to the local pub for a few more whiskeys before facing his wife.

The rain had stopped and the night was clear and crisp as he parked his car in the car park behind the pub. His hands were trembling as he ordered a double scotch. The barman cracked a joke, but Murphy did not respond, swallowing the whiskey in one gulp. He ordered another, and another. By the time he left the pub he had lost count of how much he had drunk. In his pocket he had a full half-bottle which he began to swig before starting the car.

When he reached home he drove straight into the garage. He turned the lights off, and trying to control his drunken movements, he unscrewed the top of the bottle and poured some more whiskey down his throat. Swaying slightly, he advanced on the house. It stood in darkness, and his fuddled brain tried to work out why.

Betty's! That's where Alison was. Probably weeping about me, he thought. He stumbled down the drive and turned toward his neighbor's house. Murphy leaned on the doorbell, feeling angry. Why should Alison tell Betty, anyway? It was none of her damned business.

When Betty opened the door, he pushed his way past her.

"Where is she?" he demanded.

"Who?"

"Alison. Where is she?"

"She left hours ago. She's at home," Betty glared. "You're drunk, aren't you? You should be ashamed of yourself. Going to London, having a good time, coming back drunk. . . ."

Murphy turned his back on her and staggered down the path. He reached for his bottle but remembered he had left it in the car. The garage, like the house, was still in darkness and he muttered under his breath as he fumbled with the door handle on the car.

"Good riddance," he said. "If she's gone, I can manage on my own. I can still pull the women."

He found the whiskey and slurped at it, spilling it over his chin. He stood at the garage entrance, looking up at the sloping driveway to the house, finding it increasingly difficult to remain steady.

After a moment he noticed the black shadow spilling out slowly from the larger shadow of the house.

"What the bloody hell. . . ?" he muttered, and lurched toward it. He stopped, unsteadily, and stared downward. Gradually, by the light of the street lamps, he became aware of the swarm of spiders move toward him.

"Jesus Christ!" he said stepping back incredulously. "Bloody spiders."

Like Alison, he did not like spiders, but he was not frightened of approaching, and killing, them. For a second he thought of jumping on them and crushing them. But even in his drunken state he could see there were too many for that to work.

He went back into the garage and leaned against the car. The spiders, now doubled in number, were creeping relentlessly toward him. His mind refused to work clearly; he looked around for something to scare them off with. On the shelf he saw a gallon can of gasoline.

"I'll burn the bastards," he chuckled as he lifted the can down and flipped open the safety lid. He knelt down outside the garage—the spiders only about ten feet away from him—and began to pour a thin line of gasoline in front of the advancing tide of insects. Lowering the can, he fumbled in his pockets for his matches. Finding them at last, he had difficulty in opening the box and striking one.

"I'll show you, you bloody shits," he mumbled as he finally managed to get a match lit. "I'll show you. You'll see . . . Jesus, what's that?" he yelped as he felt a sharp pain in his calf.

He looked down to see a few of the insects begin to crawl over his shoes and under his trousers.

"My God!" he screamed, and moved backward, knocking over the gas can. The fuel spread rapidly down the slope and into the garage, gathering into a pool under the car.

"Get away! Get off!" Murphy yelled, suddenly hysterical.

The lit match burned down to his trembling fingers and the pain made him drop it. A huge sheet of flame shot up in front of him and quickly raced along the spilled gasoline into the garage.

There seemed a strange moment of calm as Murphy watched the flames lick quietly around the car. Even the spiders appeared immobile. Then, suddenly realizing what was about to happen, Murphy began to run toward the hedge bordering the path.

He was too late.

There was an ear-splitting roar, and the garage disintegrated, blown outward by the exploding car. Murphy was thrown head-first into thick bushes. There he lay semiconscious.

He became gradually aware of a rippling movement over his back. Twisting his head to the side, he saw his body was covered with spiders. He felt flesh being torn from his legs. He saw a group of the insects move from a nearby bush toward his head.

The drink, the shock of the explosion, the pain in his back and legs—finally he passed out. The spiders continued to tear him to pieces, without interruption. . . .

When the police and fire brigade arrived twenty minutes later, it was to find a dead woman in the bath, her hand stripped of flesh hanging over the side. They also found a burning garage and car, and the remains of a man lying face down in the bushes, his body lacerated and torn beyond recognition.

No one took any notice of the few crushed and burnt insects scattered near the front of the garage. . . .

3

"Eaten? What the hell do you mean eaten?" Alan Mason screamed. "Inspector, people are not *eaten* in their beds in the middle of Kent."

Neil Bradshaw looked at Alan for a few seconds before replying. When the doctors had told him, he, too, could not believe it. But he had to admit that in nearly thirty years with the police he had not seen anything like the body of Dan Mason.

"Mr. Mason," he finally sighed. "We can only go by the facts. And according to preliminary reports, both from the path lab and our own doctors, your father's flesh was torn from his bones, thereby causing his death."

"Torn by what?"

The inspector shrugged.

"God knows. We found nothing. The window was open, so perhaps whatever did it got in that way. But as to clues—none. We found blood on the carpet, around the bed, and some smeared lines of blood on the windowsill. But nothing else."

Alan ran his fingers through his hair. The men were sitting downstairs in the front room of Dragon's Farm.

"I don't believe it," Alan muttered at last. "I just don't believe it."

Bradshaw was silent.

Alan had been giving a lecture at the university when the message came through from the police. His mother had been put under heavy sedation; he had driven down to Kent.

"Inspector," Alan said, raising his head. "May I see my father."

Bradshaw breathed in deeply.

"I don't know. It's not . . . it's not normal. I mean the body," he added quickly.

Alan's eyes narrowed and he clenched his teeth.

"Inspector Bradshaw," he said quietly. "I'm a scientist. A biologist. I've studied anatomy. Cut up bodies. I know what death is like. I can face it."

One hour later Alan walked out of the police morgue, his face ashen, his hands stuck deep in his pockets to hide their shaking, and staring coldly ahead. Nothing he had ever seen had prepared him for the last sight of his father.

"I'll see you later," he said as he passed Bradshaw, heading for his own car. "You were right. It's not normal."

Bradshaw watched Alan walk slowly away. The inspector had taken to him immediately. Mason was tough; you could tell that. In Bradshaw's line of business summing up people's characters came as second nature. Alan, like Dan his father, was tall. His square jaw, pale blue eyes, and close-cropped black hair gave him the look of a football player. Bradshaw got the impression that Alan was a man who could cope with life.

He waited until the car drove off, then turned back into the mortuary to find out if there were any new developments.

On sudden impulse Alan drove back to Dragon's Farm. Mentally and physically he was numbed by what he had just seen. The inspector had been right in his judgment of Alan. He took things as they came, not worrying too much about life's twists and turns. He often said that life was too short to worry, and that was why you should make the most of it. And at twenty-nine, he'd had enough experiences not to make him feel too dissatisfied.

Alan was popular at the university, with students

and professors alike. He enjoyed his pint of beer at lunch with the students as much as his formal dinners with professors and academics. In short, he was not, like so many of his colleagues, a snob.

His six-foot frame was matched by a strength that came from keen rugby training and playing and he was proud of his physical fitness.

But at that moment, driving through the peaceful countryside of Kent, he felt very weak. To think that huddle of bones smeared with blood had been his old man. He was suddenly sickened, not so much for his own sake—he knew he would survive—but for his mother. She now had nothing; her plans were destroyed. But, he thought grimly and realistically, that was a problem to deal with when she had recovered from the initial shock.

The police were still at the farmhouse when Alan arrived. As he walked through the kitchen he noticed his father's suitcase lying open on a chair.

"Who searched that?" he snapped at the nearest policeman.

"We had to, sir," the young constable replied, "in case something had been stolen."

Alan nodded and idly flicked through the clothes. They could have been a stranger's as far as he was concerned. Having been away from home for nearly eight years, seeing his parents only at weekends and during holidays, he had led his own life. What his father wore was of little relevance and so the clothes meant nothing. After all, he told himself, it was the man in them that counted.

At the bottom of the case he found a half-full bottle of brandy. He smiled. That was something else he and his father had shared. A love of drink. Not for drink's sake—Dan had instilled in him the uselessness of going over the top in anything—but for relaxation, what Dan had called "sensible drinking."

He pulled the bottle out, found a cup, and poured himself a large measure. As the warmth spread through his body, he began to feel better, and walked, cup in hand, upstairs to the bedroom.

As with the clothes, the room held no memories, so he felt nothing as he looked around. Two detectives were giving the bedroom a final check. They nodded at him and continued minutely examining the carpet.

Alan glanced at the bed, with its dark red blood stains, and then across to the open window. Going over to it, he looked down at the garden, noticing the newly dug patch. Typical, he thought fondly; Dan would live in a tent as long as he could have his garden.

He was about to turn away, when he noticed a small dark object in the corner of the outside ledge. He leaned closer to examine it. The shape of a crooked L—he smiled when he saw it was a spider's leg. The scientist in him made him automatically pick the leg up and scrutinize it closely.

Thinking he would identify it easily, Alan frowned when he found he could not.

"Interesting," he murmured. "Very interesting."

"Sorry, sir?" one of the detectives said. "Did you say something?"

Alan shook his head.

"No, no. I've just found something, that's all."

Both policemen looked at him keenly.

"Sorry," he smiled. "It's nothing of interest to you. Just a spider's leg. I'm a biologist," he explained. "These things interest me."

The detectives laughed.

"Where's the rest of it then?" one of them asked.

"Probably hiding under a stone growing another one."

"You're kidding."

"Oh, no. Spiders can amputate their legs if necessary," Alan said. "If they're in trouble, for instance.

But this one's odd. I can't make it out at all. The claws are strange," he added, peering at the leg which lay on the palm of his hand.

The detective shrugged.

"Can't see what you people find of interest in all that stuff," he said, grinning. "To me, a spider is a spider is a spider. They're all the same to me. Horrible little bastards."

Alan laughed. He did not realize it then, but he was to remember the detective's comment many times in the weeks and months to follow. . . .

Alan hung around the farmhouse for about an hour. There was nothing he could do, so after finishing the bottle of brandy he drove to the temporary headquarters which Bradshaw had set up in the nearest village.

"OK?" the inspector asked when Alan was seated in the small office which served as the police station.

He nodded.

"As well as can be expected," he replied. "Anything new?"

"Nope," Bradshaw shook his head. "Oh, yes! I'm sorry. There's one thing, but I can't make sense of it. The pathologist found a lot of poison around and on the remains of the body."

"Poison?" Alan repeated sharply. "What kind?"

"No idea," Bradshaw sighed.

Alan stared at him.

"The latest theory is that your father was subjected to some kind of poison which literally ate his flesh away," Bradshaw continued. "I don't know," he said, shaking his head. "The whole thing doesn't make any sense to me at all."

"What about the blood on the windowsill?" Alan asked.

"Your father could have crawled to the window for some reason."

"And then gone back to bed?" Alan objected. "I can't see it. I'm not a policeman, but it doesn't fit."

Bradshaw nodded.

"Exactly. It doesn't fit."

The inspector felt tired and looked it. He had been up since six o'clock that morning, when the first call came through. A farm laborer, passing and seeing the bedroom light on, had called the police, thinking tramps or squatters had taken over the empty house. The laborer had known the house was for sale—the notice had not yet been removed—and he had read somewhere what could happen to properties left empty.

The police had arrived just before 5:30 A.M., and Bradshaw had been notified not long after. He rubbed his eyes, thinking of the long, hot bath he was going to take when he returned home. Now in his late forties, Bradshaw had turned down senior posts in London in order to head the local CID in Kent. He enjoyed the lack of pressure, the chance to get to know many of the residents, as well as having the time to become involved with grass-roots problems. A fraction taller than Alan, he was beginning to thin on top, but his long, gaunt face revealed a strength of character that gained respect from his men and the public alike. His large hands, and the fact that his clothes always seemed a couple of inches too short, gave the impression of an awkward, gangling man. But Alan had the feeling that, when the cards were stacked, the inspector could be as tough and sharp as honed steel.

Now the inspector was nonplussed. Even in the most difficult cases, cases which Bradshaw had pursued relentlessly, there had been at least *one* clue. But Dan Mason's case had him totally baffled. And it was this, besides the lack of sleep, which made him feel weary and defeated.

"What happens now?" Alan asked.

"We continue investigating. We speak to everyone in

the area. Who saw your father? When? What was he doing? Did he seem to be fit? And so on. The usual stuff," he commented, feeling that he could open up to Alan. "Quite frankly, Alan, this is a stinker. To be honest, I don't know what the hell we can do now."

Alan grunted. "Well, maybe something'll turn up." He was surprised that he was not more angry; surprised that he had actually offered some sort of consolation to the inspector. But Alan was impressed by the man's open honesty, his treatment of him as an adult, thinking person, not just another member of the public to be fobbed off somehow.

"If there's anything more, I'll be . . ."

Alan was interrupted by the phone. Bradshaw snatched it up to his ear.

"Yes?" he said curtly, holding his other hand up to Alan, indicating for him to stay.

"What? Where? Right, I'll be there in ten minutes." He put the phone down and looked at Alan.

"It's impossible. Bloody impossible!" he emphasized, banging his fist on the desk top.

Alan sat still, waiting.

"There's been a fire. Two deaths," the inspector went on. "But not because of the fire. They found the woman in the bath and the man outside in the garden. The local sergeant says it looks as if they've both been eaten. Flesh torn from their bodies."

Bradshaw began to rise.

"I must get over there. I'll see you later," he said.

"Can I join you?" Alan asked impulsively, not quite sure why he had offered.

Bradshaw hesitated for a few moments.

"OK, come on," he agreed. "A scientific mind might help."

They drove in silence, reaching the next village within a few minutes. Police cars were parked in the driveway of the Murphys' home, and a fire engine stood beside the smoldering garage, which firemen were spraying with foam.

Alan and Bradshaw walked over to the sergeant in charge.

"Where are the bodies?" Bradshaw asked curtly.

"There's one over in those bushes, and the other's upstairs in the bath," the sergeant told him.

"You can stay here if you want," the inspector said, turning to Alan. "I've got to look at them—it's my job."

Alan shook his head, and they walked across to where the body of John Murphy lay covered by a ground sheet.

A policeman pulled the sheet back. The corpse was every bit as hideous as his father's had been. Alan turned away, almost retching.

He followed Bradshaw to the bathroom, where the body of Alison Murphy, her face contorted by fear and drowning, lay with one arm over the edge. Or what was left of her arm.

The inspector began piecing together the story of the discovery. Alan, feeling useless, wandered outside toward the garage. The firemen had almost finished, so he skirted around the charred remains. Finding a low wall he sat down, his head bowed, pondering on what he had seen.

He leaped up suddenly. On the concrete before him he had noticed a dark fragment similar to the one he had seen on the window ledge at Dragon's Farm. He picked it up. Another spider's leg, but this time larger and thicker—and the bristles harder. The claws at the base of the four-part hinged limb were almost flat, the two powerful pincers obviously suited to running as well as clinging.

He looked around for more, but the firemen and policemen had trampled the area near the garage into a muddy mess, so he found nothing.

Alan went back into the house and examined his discovery under the light. He did not hear Bradshaw come up behind him and peer round, curious to know what Alan was looking at.

"Bloody scientists!" the inspector said.

Alan spun around.

"Do you never stop?" Bradshaw asked with a faint smile. "Two grisly murders in one day, and you're studying spiders' legs! A world of your own, that's what you scientists live in. A world of your own."

Alan nodded, his face blank and serious, not daring to voice the terrible theory forming at the edge of his mind. . . .

4

By the time she was sixteen, Suzy Carter was fully developed. On the day she left school she had flung her uniform in the garbage, bought some new clothes, and dyed her hair blonde. Then she went to her local supermarket—one of two in the small town in Kent—and immediately got herself a job as a checkout girl.

The job was only a fill-in as far as Suzy was concerned. She was determined to go to London, where the real money was to be made. As soon as she had earned enough, then she would pack and be off to the city. For Suzy was an ambitious girl, with an eye to the fashion world, the glitter of the glossy magazines, the fantasy of television commercials featuring gorgeous women on private yachts. Suzy felt that she was just as beautiful as the girls she saw in these ads. And in some ways she was right.

Her skin was pale, soft, and unblemished. Makeup on it was really an insult, though she was too young to realize that, and she tended to wear too much lipstick, eye shadow, and mascara. The eyes, deep blue and bright, gave her an innocent look, which to most men was unnerving, to most boys complimentary. Her lips, though small, were set in a perpetual sensual pout, and her nose was small and rounded. It was almost a perfect face.

Her breasts were not large, but well proportioned for her five-foot-three body. Suzy thought her best point was her legs. They were beautifully shaped, tapering down from a deceptively slim waist and hips.

All in all, Suzy was a beautiful young woman. She

had everything Nature could have given her. Except experience.

But by the time she was sixteen and a half she was beginning to achieve it. For Suzy had taken a lover. A man who made her feel like a woman, she said. A man who had seen the world, who had traveled to France and Italy. A man who uncovered her innermost sensual and sexual desires. Brought them to the surface and satisfied them.

Suzy's was a secret affair. It had to be secret. For her lover was a local schoolteacher—one of the teachers who had taught her. David Pringle by name, Suzy's lover was in his late twenties. His wife was a few years younger.

Every Saturday, Pringle did his duty going shopping in the supermarket, and it was over a basketful of tinned and packaged food that love first blossomed. Two months after they met again, Suzy and Pringle consummated their ripening love in the back of his Ford Anglia.

Suzy saw the affair as an adventure, a thrill. And if they had to meet in secret, that was just fine. She actually believed she was in love. An adult love, a mature woman's love. For did not Pringle prefer her to his wife?

Suzy began to reveal her new confidence in herself through an arrogance to her friends and parents. She ignored her father's few complaints about her returning late, disregarded her mother's pleas to dress sensibly. What did *they* know, after all?

And as she pulled on her tights that warm autumn night, she looked forward to the evening ahead because she was meeting her lover later in the woods on the outskirts of town. As Suzy slipped into a cotton dress she smiled at her own wickedness in leaving her panties off. David Pringle was a man who did not like to waste time.

She flounced downstairs and poked her head round the living-room door.

"I'm off," she said to her parents, who were watching television.

"Don't be late," her father said, his eyes never leaving the screen.

"Are you dressed properly?" her mother asked, glancing up.

"Perfectly," Suzy said, and closed the door behind her.

The night was clear and a full moon hung low in the sky. Walking along the dimly lit street, she wondered if the stories about people going mad at the time of the full moon were true. Quickening her step, she hurried along the deserted road and soon reached the outskirts of town.

Here the bright moon flung the long shadows of hedges and trees across the rough path that led into the woods looming darkly ahead. Suzy suddenly shivered, and then caught her breath sharply as a twig snapped somewhere inside the woods. Suzy did not like the dark and wondered why she had ever agreed to meet David at night, but when they had made love there once during the summer, everything seemed different, less threatening.

She glanced up at the moon. It hung white as a skull, and to Suzy it now seemed menacing—not romantic as it had been on that summer evening. She walked forward slowly into the shady darkness, ripples of uncertainty moving down her back.

Inside the woods the light was gray and the tall trees seemed to press down around her. A scuffle and a squawk to her right made her cry out, but, realizing that it must have been only a bird, she told herself not to be silly.

At last she reached their meeting place, a clearing with a large spreading oak tree in the center. She ran across the open space and stood under the tree, bitterly disappointed that David had not arrived first. Suzy stood perfectly still, clutching her handbag and listening for her lover's footsteps. All she heard were the night sounds of the woods—the creaking timbers, the animals in the undergrowth, and the occasional muted cry of a bird disturbed in its nest.

Please, please come soon, David. Oh, God make him come soon, she prayed. *I'm frightened. I don't like the dark.* She strained her ears, desperate for his footsteps, his voice. Nothing, except the noises of the night. And something more. A sort of indistinct rustling that was difficult to pinpoint. A sliding, scraping, almost whispering sound.

She looked up at the moon, saw its grim, twisted smile, and thought of the tales she had heard. Her heart pounded.

Oh God, David, where are you?

When she heard the crunching of twigs she began to shake. It came from behind her, but Suzy could not, dare not, turn.

"Sorry I'm a few minutes late, darling," she heard David's voice.

Turning, she flung herself into his arms, half sobbing, half laughing with relief.

"Hey, hey," he said softly. "You're shaking. What's wrong?"

"The dark. . . . I don't like the dark," Suzy stuttered. "I'm frightened."

"There now," he said, holding her close. "It's all right."

Cupping her chin in his hand, he tilted her head upward and kissed her gently on the lips. The warmth of his lips, the pressure of his body, the strong emotions let loose by her fear, made Suzy want David desperately. She pulled him slowly to the ground. He stopped her for a moment, slipped off his sheepskin coat and laid it out on the damp grass.

Clinging tightly to him, Suzy felt his strong, firm hands run over her body, aware of his hardness against her stomach. Closing her eyes she moved her hips round in a circular motion against his manhood. David began to moan and she opened her eyes to watch his face, a pale rounded face with small eyes, a large thin-lipped mouth, and a shock of fair hair. His mouth was slightly open—and then he gasped as he quickly came.

Suzy gave a deep, throaty chuckle and, shifting her position, slid her hand down to his trousers. She quickly and expertly unzipped them, frantically pulling his underpants away from the object of her heated desire.

Pringle stood up and quickly stripped. Suzy lay, her skirt hitched up past her waist, watching him. He knelt in front of her, and kissed her between the legs, his hands pulling down her tights. Suzy panted aloud as her excitement mounted.

Soon he was astride her, and she cried out with relief as she felt him enter her. A slight breeze sprang up, and she opened her eyes and watched the trees move slightly in the wind. She thought she saw a leaf gliding downward directly above them, but thought no more of it as David's hands caressed her breasts.

He paused and took one hand away from her.

"Bloody leaves," he said, as he twisted his hand round to his back and brushed something off.

She clasped her hands behind his neck, pulling him even closer. Something tickled the back of her hand and she shook it off. A quick thought about not making love again outside crossed her mind.

As Suzy neared orgasm she lifted her hands from Pringle's back and, spreading her fingers, pressed her palms into the cool, damp earth. Her head rolled to one side and she was lost in a tumultuous wave of passion.

Then she heard Pringle scream but, assuming that he was coming too, she raised her body to meet him. But Pringle had suddenly stopped thrusting, though his screams became louder and more piercing. She opened her eyes, her head still turned sideways.

A knot of panic formed in her stomach. A few feet from her face, quivering in the cold light of the full moon, stood a spider larger than any she had ever seen. Its eight eyes were staring unblinkingly at them.

"David! David!" she cried, instinctively pulling her hands in to her sides.

David Pringle was writhing wildly on top of her, and she quickly turned her head toward him. At first she could not make out what was happening. The full moon was almost obliterated by hundreds of dark shapes floating down from the branches of the huge oak tree above them.

As her eyes focused in the gloom, Suzy began to shriek with terror. Hanging from invisible threads, a cloud of spiders was falling quickly onto Pringle's back. She felt a tug at her hair. Her hand shot up and grasped the squirming bristly body of a spider. Flinging it away, she tried to move from under her lover's twisting, thrashing, body. But she was trapped; he was too heavy. Looking desperately around, she saw a black mass, like a spearhead of lava, break from some nearby bushes and advance rapidly over the ground toward them.

Then suddenly Pringle shot away from her—and she staggered to her feet, falling back against the trunk of the tree. She watched, her throat constricted with terror, as her lover stumbled across the clearing, his back almost covered by a mass of frantic spiders. He fell, and rolled over on his back, still screaming; but the insects already on the ground quickly clambered over his naked chest and belly, biting, tearing, pulling at his exposed flesh.

Suzy felt something move across her foot. She looked down. A spider was beginning to crawl up her leg. Sweeping it away with her hand she plunged blindly into the woods. Fighting her way through the undergrowth, her dress caught and ripped by the bushes, she ran sobbing until she finally collapsed by the side of a small stream.

From behind her, Pringle's screams grew to a crescendo—and then, in the middle of a long howl, they stopped abruptly. The silence fell like a solid blanket around her. Nothing moved in the darkness. Suzy looked about her. Sensing something stir in the trees above her, she glanced up just as the first dark shape began to fall.

She got up and began to run along the bank of the stream. Her stomach twisted with fear. A few hundred yards on, she fell again, nearly all energy gone. She looked back. Nothing. She felt she could not move, but when something hit her on the face, she clawed at it wildly. A leaf crumbled in her hand. Blood began to trickle from the long scratch on her cheek, received from a lashing briar.

Suzy had lost all sense of direction, but instinct drove her forward. Dragging her feet over the muddy embankment, she staggered away from the horror behind her. Every sound from the black woods, every twig that snapped, every bird that squealed, every rustle of the branches around her, added another dimension of terror and panic.

And all the time she saw that grotesque image before her—spiders crawling over her naked lover's body. She could still feel the bristly insect she had pulled from her hair, its jagged legs digging into her palm. Not realizing it, she kept wiping her hand on the side of her torn dress, as if to wipe away the horror of the loathsome creature.

"Spiders. Spiders. Spiders," she repeated hysterically as she ran. The remembered sight of hundreds of them moving across the clearing was almost more than her mind could stand. She hated spiders, hated the creepy way they moved, hated everything about them. The living nightmare she had experienced would haunt her life.

Eventually, she broke away from the woods into a newly furrowed field. She collapsed on the black, cold earth and sobbed convulsively, her cheek pressed against the ground. Her body felt heavy, too heavy to move. She lay there, letting the tears flow over her face, still refusing to believe what had happened.

A noise from the woods behind her snapped her into action. Stumbling across the field she came to a road. Again instinct drove her on and she ran down the empty road, silver in the ghastly light from the moon.

Ten minutes later she staggered into the outskirts of town, her torn and muddied dress flapping about her knees. There was no one about as Suzy ran through the streets, gasping for breath, her eyes bulging with fear and racked sobs breaking through the quiet of the night.

She did not hear the car draw up beside her, and was hardly aware of the hands that forced her into the back seat. A few minutes later she was helped out and up some steps into the local police station. All reality had fled and Suzy no longer knew what was happening. She felt a sharp pain across her cheek as a policeman slapped her once, and then she quieted down.

"I just found her running along the road, sergeant," a man's voice explained.

"It's young Suzy Carter," the sergeant said. "We'd better phone her parents. Looks as if she's been attacked."

"Spiders. Spiders. Spiders," Suzy mumbled, slowly beginning to realize she was safe.

"What's that, miss?" asked the sergeant, a large, bulky man.

"Spiders . . . Spiders . . . Spiders."

"Yes, yes. You're all right now," the policeman went on. "Here's a cup of tea," he said, laying a cup on a table before her.

They were in the small interview room to the side of the main entrance to the police station, and the constable who had brought the tea asked if he should phone her parents.

"Go ahead," the sergeant told him. "Tell them she's been in an accident. Don't give any details until we can find out what happened."

Suzy stared ahead, her lips moving rapidly, making indistinct sounds.

"Now, miss, can you tell us about it?"

Suzy shook her head from side to side, still mumbling incoherently.

"I think you'd better leave now," the sergeant said to the man who had brought Suzy in. "Perhaps she doesn't want to talk in front of you. Oh, and Bill," he added as the man went to leave, "see the man on the desk before you go, and give him the details."

Suddenly Suzy started screaming, her body shaking uncontrollably. The sergeant slapped her once again and this time Suzy stopped rigid though her eyes darted around like a frightened dog's.

A policewoman came into the room.

"I was told you might need me," she said. "What's happened?"

The sergeant shrugged.

"She won't say."

Suzy began to speak.

"Spiders. Big spiders," she whispered. "Thousands of them. All over. Eating David. All over him. Eaten by them. Big spiders. David dead. Dead . . . Aaaaah!" she ended in a scream.

The policewoman and the sergeant looked at each other and shrugged. Suzy kept wiping her hand against her side.

"Spiders?" the woman said. "Spiders attacked you and your boyfriend? Where?"

"In the woods. The woods. Thousands of them. Big spiders. Big spiders. Eating David. Eating . . ." her voice trailed off into a mumble.

The sergeant sighed, and leaned over to the woman.

"Her mind's gone, obviously. Carnivorous spiders! Poor kid. She must have had some experience," he said in a low voice. "Do you think she's been raped?"

The policewoman nodded.

"Why don't you leave me alone with her and I'll try to find out?" she asked.

The sergeant left.

"And now, Suzy," the woman began, "let's have no more nonsense about spiders. If someone attacked you, tell me about it. We want to catch him before he does it again."

"Spiders. Spiders. In the woods. Big spiders. Eating David. David dead. David dead. Oh no," she broke down, weeping loudly.

The policewoman stayed with Suzy for nearly half an hour. Her parents had arrived and were waiting outside. Finally the woman gave up and went out to talk to the sergeant.

"She's still saying it was spiders that attacked her and her boyfriend—this David, whoever he is. And she keeps rubbing her hand against her leg. I would call in the doctor and put her under sedation. Maybe she'll talk sense tomorrow."

"The doctor's already here," the sergeant said. "Did she say which woods?"

"I think it's the ones about half a mile from her house."

"We'd better take a look. If she has been raped—and the doctor'll be able to tell us soon—then maybe the bastard who did it left some clues." The sergeant grunted. "Spiders! That's a new one. Probably doesn't want her parents to know she was in the woods. From what I hear, she's a right little tease," he added disapprovingly. "Well, let's move. I'll go with Constable Jones. Two of us should be enough. I'd better take some fly-killer in case we come across some giant flies," he laughed.

But the sergeant was not laughing one hour later as he stood in the woods watching a police photographer take shots of the unsightly remains of David Pringle's body. Chunks of Pringle's flesh had been torn off, and raw, still dripping coils of the young schoolteacher's intestines extruded limply from the naked corpse.

But it was not only the sight of the body which caused Sergeant Wilkies so much concern and made him feel a little frightened. For next to the body, on the flattened grass, lay the crushed remains of a spider. It was larger than any he had ever seen.

5

Alan stayed in Kent on the Monday night after the Murphys were discovered. He drank heavily and ate little. Finding the people in the hotel bar boring, he went to his room, where he slowly made his way through most of a bottle of brandy. Every twenty minutes or so he would pull out an envelope and empty the spiders' legs he had discovered on to a coffee table, peering at them intently.

"I wonder . . . I wonder," he kept repeating, tapping his long slim fingers on the table.

He had a bath and went to bed early, hoping that the alcohol would give him the benefit of sleep. But he was kept awake thinking about the spiders' legs. There was something familiar about them, and yet they were not normal. Once back in London he would be able to check. Just before he drifted off, he remembered that he had not phoned Louise or his mother. Ah well, he would be returning first thing in the morning.

He woke just before noon the next day. His head thumped and his body ached. At first he wondered if the whole thing had been a drunken nightmare, but the sight of the envelope on the coffee table brought him back to reality.

After a shower, a shave, and a pot of hot, black coffee, he felt better. He put through his calls to London. His mother was still under sedation. Louise said she would be at her apartment and they arranged to meet there later. Alan next called Inspector Bradshaw.

"Anything new on the Murphys?" he asked.

"No. It's the same as your father. The pathology boys found poison around the bodies again, by the way. It's got me screwed up. I'm wondering when the next murder will be."

"Let me know if you find anything," Alan said. "I'm going back to London. I'll be in touch."

He gave the inspector his own and Louise's number.

He reached London around three o'clock and went straight to his laboratory at the university. There he examined the spiders' legs under a microscope, checking the structure with Kaestner's classification, the standard work on *Araneida*—spiders. And then he double-checked—for he could not believe what he had found.

He ran his hands through his hair, a habit of his when perplexed. Feeling he needed another expert opinion, he called his friend Peter Whitley in the Natural History Department, a leading expert on insects. After Whitley had studied the legs, he turned to Alan, a puzzled expression on his face.

"You said you found these here, in this country?" he queried. "It's impossible."

"That's what I thought. But they came from Kent."

"Did someone give them to you?"

Alan shook his head.

"No. Without going into lengthy detail, I found the legs separately, say, three or four miles apart from each other."

Alan did not want to tell Whitley the full circumstances in case his friend thought him crazy.

"These legs look as if they belong to a *Stegodyphus*," Whitley went on. "But this species of spider lives only in Pakistan. And they hunt in groups, hundreds of them in one pack. If you found these in this country, the chances are high that there must be more."

Alan raised his eyebrows. "Brilliant. I'll put you in for the Nobel Prize. But Peter," Alan continued seriously. "Look at the claws at the foot of each leg.

They're not Stegodyphus. They look as if they're geared to running, not clinging to webs. And the bristles—they're far too hard for our Pakistani monster."

Whitley raised his hands and shrugged. He was a small man who looked like the stereotype of a scientist. His clothes were always crumpled, and he had even been known to wear one black shoe and one brown to a college dinner. His rounded face was almost lost in the shock of curly fair hair, and a shaggy brown beard.

But he was brilliant, and Alan's joke about the Nobel Prize was not totally inappropriate.

"You're right," he said. "All this talk about Stegodyphus—it's crazy! Of course you can't have a Pakistani spider wandering around in Kent." He nodded vigorously. "And there *are* differences. You've got to remember, Alan, that the Kaestner classification, good though it is, only scratches the surface. There must be thousands and thousands of species we don't know about. New types are being found almost every day. This could be one of them. And you know as well as I do that you can't get an accurate identification from one leg. So don't get too excited."

Alan was not convinced. He clasped his hands, rubbing the palms together.

"You do agree, Peter," he said slowly, "that these legs *look* like Stegodyphus from Pakistan?"

"Yes, yes," Whitley answered, becoming irritated and tugging lightly at his beard. "But this is stupid. If they did come from Stegodyphus, then someone would have seen them. These buggers run around in packs of hundreds—sometimes thousands."

Alan grunted, and sighed deeply.

"I suppose you're right. But . . . but assuming there were a few floating about. What would they live off?"

Whitley shook his head.

"No idea. Spiders need live food," he said. "If they

don't get that they'll eat each other. My guess is that you've probably found the remains of our hairy friend after he's come across in a packing case. Remember the fuss about the so-called Red Killer Spider they thought had come to Britain in a load of bananas?"

Alan nodded.

"Why were the legs found so far apart, then, genius?"

"A bird probably picked it up. It might have pecked at the spider in one spot and flown with it to another. How the hell do I know?"

Alan rubbed his eyes with the heels of his palms.

"You look tired, Alan," Peter smiled. "Been out on the town again?"

"No, it's not that," Alan replied flatly. "My father was killed yesterday."

Whitley blinked in disbelief.

"Your . . . Jesus! I'm sorry," he stuttered. "I had no idea. Killed? How?"

Alan stared at Whitley for a few moments, a strange smile playing around his lips.

"Spiders," he said quietly, shocked at the sound of his own voice actually saying it.

Louise was waiting at her place, as she had promised. She stood to one side as he walked in and along the narrow hall. She did not know him well enough yet to judge how the shock of his father's death had affected him. He went straight into the living room. Louise lived on her own in a modern one-bed-room apartment.

Alan slouched down on a cord easy chair. Louise stood by the door, waiting.

"Come here, you silly thing," he smiled. "I'm not going to start crying or anything like that."

He held his arms out and she flung herself at him,

burying her head in his chest. He smelled her sweet perfume and ran his fingers through her red hair.

"I feel so helpless," she murmured. "I don't know what to do . . . what to say."

"You can get me a drink for a start," he chuckled.

She stood up and padded softly across to a white wood sideboard. She pulled out a bottle of whiskey and two glasses. Alan watched her concentrate on pouring the drinks.

She was not a classical beauty, but as Alan said she had "natural" appeal, an indefinable quality which attracted men to her. At first he thought it had been her eyes, green and always laughing—though they could become troubled instantly when she was worried, particularly about her friends.

She was small—just over five foot—and well proportioned. If her breasts were on the small side, at least there was no hint of sagging, as she often joked to Alan. Her stomach was flat, although she did not follow any special diet. Her thighs were trim, too, even if she did not have perfectly sculptured legs.

Louise was not the sort of girl who worried about such things. Her hair was soft, red, and shoulder-length, and she generally fixed it herself, thinking hairdressers rather a waste of time. But when she did visit one, she was always thrilled. Almost like a little girl. Natural.

"Ice in your whiskey?" she asked, turning to him, her hair bouncing with the movement.

Alan shook his head, and Louise brought the glasses across. She sat at his feet, leaning against his legs.

They remained like that for nearly half an hour, slowly sipping their drinks. From time to time Alan rubbed his hand gently over Louise's shoulder. She did not question him. She knew he would speak when he wanted to, and there was no point in forcing him.

As the light faded, Alan began to tell her of what he

had found and seen. When he had finished, she twisted round and laid her hand on his. By the light of the street lamps he saw her eyes troubled and tear-filled. He knew he wanted her that moment more than ever before.

Louise stood up and, cupping her small hand in his, she gently pulled him to his feet. In silence she led him to the bedroom, where they made love softly and gently. Afterwards, Louise curled up against him, and Alan marveled yet again at the softness of her skin and her radiating warmth. His hand cupped one breast, the nipple pressing into his palm.

In that position they fell asleep.

Alan was wakened by the shrill ringing of the phone. He leaned across Louise, who was stirring out of sleep. Before picking up the receiver he glanced at the bedside clock. It was 7 A.M.

"Yes? Who the hell is it?" he barked.

"Bradshaw. Sorry to call you so early. But there's been another development."

Alan was immediately awake.

"What's happened?" he asked.

"Another body. This time four miles from the Murphys' place. A man in a wood. But this time we've got a witness," the inspector added curtly. "And something we can't explain."

"Go on," Alan said impatiently.

"His girlfriend says they were attacked by . . . I know it sounds ridiculous, but she says they were attacked by *spiders*!"

Alan stiffened. "Is that what you can't explain?" he asked hoarsely.

"No. We found a dead spider near the body. A big one," Bradshaw said. "It's crushed, but you're a biologist and maybe you can make something of it. It's on the way to your lab at the moment."

Alan felt Louise's hand move around his stomach and he gently moved it away.

"Inspector," he said quietly. "I think I'd better come down and have a talk with you. I'll arrange to have the spider examined. I hope to God I'm wrong, and you might want to have me certified as insane after I tell you what I'm beginning to think."

"What do you mean 'beginning to think'?"

"Just what I say. It's a half-formed, half-baked shred of an idea. Too crazy for words at this stage, perhaps, but I'll tell you when I see you."

He called Peter Whitley and instructed him to examine the spider and phone the results through to Kent, giving him Bradshaw's number. He gulped down a cup of coffee before leaving and told Louise he would be in touch.

Alan could not know it, but as he drove into Kent, events were taking place which would turn his shadowy theory into incontrovertible fact. . . .

6

Wednesday morning started like any other for the Grants. Jimmy Grant moaned about the lack of mail. His wife Sheila moaned at Jimmy's moans, saying that they had come down from Scotland to escape mail and telephones. Their three-year-old son Damien refused to eat his breakfast, demanding candy instead. When Jimmy gave his son a small bar of chocolate, Sheila stomped out of the room screaming about "irresponsible attitudes and obese children." And then their seven-month-old baby daughter, Tricia, began crying for more milk.

Sheila was in the process of feeding the baby when Jimmy poked his head around the door and shouted, "Irresponsible parent! Do you want a fat baby?"

It was, in short, a normal morning for the Grants.

The family had only been in Tunbridge Wells a few weeks. Jimmy was a senior lecturer in History at Aberdeen University, and Sheila, nearly ten years younger in her early twenties, had been one of his students. Despite the noisy arguments and slanging matches which they indulged in nearly every day, they basically enjoyed each other's company.

Jimmy was on his sabbatical year. At first he had been at a loss for what to do with the time.

"You do realize the theory of a sabbatical year, Mr. Grant?" his professor had asked him sternly.

"Certainly, sir," Jimmy had replied. "It's to allow us to do some research and keep up to date with the latest books." he went on, wondering if he could afford to spend six months in southern Spain.

"Well, I look forward to seeing an exciting paper at the end of your year," the professor nodded seriously.

"Of course, sir."

Jimmy left the professor's office, went to the local pub, booked a room, and a few days later held a going-away party which was still being talked about three months after the event.

As far as a paper was concerned, Jimmy and the other lecturers knew that the old professor had been saying the same thing to those going on sabbaticals for at least twenty years. And no one had returned with an original piece of research yet. The majority of them came back with suntans and an increased knowledge of mountain climbing or some other favored pastime. But research? Never. Most people thought a sabbatical year too precious to waste on work.

The Grants had finally decided Spain was not a good idea, the baby being so young, and the water out there supposedly full of strange bacteria. Jimmy was disappointed, because he had never been to Spain. But Sheila, a hard-headed woman, would not be persuaded.

"What's wrong with going down to Kent and visiting all our friends there that you're always moaning about not seeing?" she asked. "And if we choose a good spot we can get up to London and see some shows."

"Strip shows?" Jimmy smiled.

Sheila raised her eyebrows in mock disgust.

But to Kent they had gone, a friend finding a cheap property on the outskirts of Tunbridge Wells. The owners had gone abroad for a year and basically wanted someone in the house to keep squatters out.

It was a large, rambling building with a huge garden extending all around it. The house was too big for Sheila to cope with, but luckily the owners' regular cleaning lady had agreed to pop in every afternoon to help out. Given the fact that the old lady was crazy about babies, the Grants seemed to have struck gold—so Jimmy put it.

"Old Mrs. Thing'll love to babysit when we go up

to London," he told Sheila. He was right. Mrs. Jenkins—Jimmy refused to call her by her correct
name—was only too pleased to stay the night while
Jimmy and Sheila tripped the sites fantastic in London.

On the afternoon of the "obese children" argument,
Jimmy decided that he *had* better do some reading, so
he disappeared into the study upstairs with a copy of
Historical Quarterly and immersed himself in the alternatives facing Elizabeth I and her overseas territories.
He was so engrossed in this gripping piece of historical
guesswork that he soon fell asleep.

Sheila puttered around downstairs for a while, playing with Damien. She put him to bed for a nap around
three o'clock. The children shared a downstairs bedroom that overlooked the back garden. Damien attempted to crawl out of bed three times before he stuck
his thumb in his mouth and curled up, looking
reproachfully at his mother.

The baby was fast asleep, and Sheila quietly closed
the door behind her before going into the kitchen to
start preparing the evening meal. She turned the radio
on and was soon listening intently to a gripping play.

Damien did not go to sleep. Making occasional gur-
gling noises he lay watching the trees through the open
window. He chuckled when he saw two birds swing out
of the branches, twittering noisily in the autumn sun.

He laughed when he saw a black spider crawl over
the window ledge, pause, and then move forward over
the sill and on to the inside ledge. It prompted a
childish memory from one of his nursery-rhyme books.

He sat up, taking his thumb out of his mouth.

"Piedah, piedah," he chortled, remembering his
mother reading him the story of Little Miss Muffet.

Damien watched fascinated as more and more spiders appeared on the window ledge and quickly poured
into the room. He laughed aloud as they scuttled over
the carpet and then stopped, a thick black ribbon spread-

ing from the window into the center of the bedroom, cutting a path between the baby's cot and Damien's bed.

"Piedah, piedah," he repeated as he leaned over the edge of his bed, innocent eyes watching the insects which now stood immobile. He did not know what to make of the particularly large black creature that had appeared at the window. It looked like a spider but, even with Damien's limited concept of size, he could see it was bigger. He watched, a smile on his face, as the big one raised two legs in the air, waving them from side to side. Damien saw the sun glint on the big one's scaly fangs at the base of its biting jaws, and he laughed at the moving light.

He did not notice the band of spiders on the floor split into two columns, one moving toward the cot, the other toward him. He was watching the light play on the big one's fangs. He only stopped laughing when the first few black insects slid smoothly over the edge of his bed and darted across the coverlet.

A few inches away from Damien the lead spiders paused for a second in their onward flow, and then one jumped on to the child's arm. Damien felt a sharp pain. Other creatures began to swarm over the child. He was now screaming.

In the kitchen Sheila sensed, rather than heard, her son's screams. She turned the radio off and the child's terrified cries pierced the sudden silence.

Fear making her heart pound heavily, she rushed to the bedroom and flung the door open. The room was a seething mass of black, and scores of insects continued to cascade from the window in a lumpy flow. The small bed was covered. She could see only the top of Damien's head and one arm under the solid, moving, hideous mound of spiders.

Aghast she turned to the cot and saw hundreds of seething spiders scrambling over each other and the baby inside. Sheila screamed, short repetitive screams, as she stumbled forward.

"Damien! Tricia! Oh, God! . . . Jimmy! Jimmy!" she yelled as she tried to reach the cot, her feet crunching on hard-backed insects as she made her way forwards. She did not spot the larger creature moving to the left of her foot. But she felt it. Glancing quickly down she saw the freak spider pull its poison fangs out of her leg. Its black hairy body and unblinking eyes recreated every horror of spiders she'd had since a child, and she tried to scream even louder; but her throat refused to respond and a choking, gasping sound came out instead. She lurched away from it but already a troop of the smaller insects were scurrying up her bare legs, biting, pulling, ripping.

She tripped and fell forward, then the final scream came—a long, primeval wail which woke Jimmy upstairs and brought him rushing down.

For Sheila it was too late. When she fell and saw the dark bristly bodies swarming around her, her mind exploded and the stress put on her heart finally caused it to burst.

At this point Jimmy reached the door. First he could not register what was happening. And then, through the swirling, mud-like blackness on the floor, he discerned the body of his wife.

Instinctively he looked toward Damien's bed, and what he saw there took every ounce of strength from him. His stomach heaved and he felt sickly bile rising in his throat.

Jimmy returned his horrified gaze to the floor and saw the spiders now advancing toward him. In the center of the oncoming tide sat two huge spiders, much bigger than crabs, with turtle-like backs.

Jimmy could not move. His legs felt like lead and he had no strength even to drag himself away. He felt impotent as the first spiders crawled over his shoes and under the legs of his pants. He became aware of the stinging, nipping, needlesharp bites of countless fangs and felt blood ooze down his leg.

And as the giant spiders began their obscene, swaying advance towards him, the other smaller insects left Sheila's body, exposing her to his horrified gaze. Jimmy could take no more. He slumped down unconscious, and the spiders continued their ghastly feast, until they, too, could take no more and slid silently back through the window.

At that moment Mrs. Jenkins was walking around the side of the house, a load of food and some sweets for the children in the basket hanging from her arm. Mrs. Jenkins never used the front door but came in through the ever-open kitchen entrance at the back.

She turned the corner of the house to see the black stream of spiders spilling out of the children's nursery toward the foot of the garden. She dropped her basket and watched, transfixed, as the seemingly endless file of insects marched away, their thick legs dancing across the grass and vegetable patches.

It was the dawning realization of what she was watching—a horde of full-bodied, evil-looking spiders—that snapped her out of her trance. She ran back to the main street, her face white with fear, and almost collapsed into the phone booth at the end of the road. There she dialed 999 and asked for the police before breaking into hysterics.

She was still in the phone booth when the police arrived. Between fits of uncontrollable sobbing, she told them what she had seen. By that time, however, Inspector Bradshaw had arrived and seen for himself the carnage in the children's bedroom.

His face was grim as he came out of the house. He was carrying a small, black plastic bag inside which were the crushed bodies of three spiders that had been found under the mangled corpse of Sheila Grant.

7

Alan Mason looked down at the three specimens the inspector had laid out on the Grants' kitchen table.

"There's no doubt now," Bradshaw said. "These little bastards are responsible for the deaths. We've even got a witness, though she's now halfway to the nuthouse herself. Still, if what she says is true, that's not surprising."

"Mmmm," murmured Alan, turning one of the bodies over. "They're not so little. Unbelievable, absolutely unbelievable," he added straightening up.

"What do you make of it?" the inspector asked.

"God knows. I've never seen anything like it before," he said, sitting down heavily and putting the dead creatures back in the polythene bag. He sighed. "This confirms my worst fears. When I found these two legs at the other victims' houses, legs which were difficult to identify, I still couldn't accept that there was some kind of flesh-eating spider on the loose. But that's what I was going to tell you, when you phoned, though I thought you'd tell me I was crazy."

Bradshaw did not comment. If anyone had indeed told him that morning that there was an army of man-eating spiders on the loose in Kent, he *would* have thought them mad.

"Mrs. Jenkins," Alan said. "What did she say exactly?"

"She's in a terrible way, you must remember," the inspector replied. "The doctor's given her something to calm her down, but she's in a hopeless state of shock. She kept muttering about *millions* of spiders crawling away from the house. Is that possible?"

"It's probably an exaggeration. But I'll say this," he emphasized, eyeing the policeman directly. "There must have been one hell of a lot of them to wipe out a family of four."

Bradshaw stared at Alan.

"Oh, Jesus!" exclaimed Alan suddenly, his eyes closing.

"What is it?"

"Breeding," he said quietly. "They'll be breeding. Got to be. And you know what that means."

The inspector shook his head slowly.

"Female spiders can produce egg sacs with anything from a few to a thousand eggs in each. And if they're on the move they'll be establishing sorts of colonies where the young can hatch safely. And the chances of finding them are fairly remote, I would say, unless . . ."

"What?" Bradshaw asked sharply.

"Unless the females are like the wolf spider and carry their egg sacs around attached to their spinnerets—things at the back of a spider which produce the silk for webs." Alan paused. "If that is the case, then we're really in trouble. They'll just go on breeding, and spreading out at the same time."

"Bloody hell."

"Exactly," Alan said. "But it may not be as bad as that. I'll get these specimens back to the lab and make a proper examination with a colleague of mine. We should be in a better position to tell you more by tomorrow."

"Will they strike again?"

Alan shrugged. "I can't say. They may have gone back to their lair, or be hiding in some woods. I don't know. There's not that much we know about ordinary spiders, as it is, never mind this type of monster," he pointed out.

Alan left to drive back to London, after phoning Louise and asking her to meet him at the lab with Peter Whitley. As he drove up the M2, with a police car in front flashing its lights to clear the traffic—something Bradshaw had insisted on—he pondered the full implications of what he had been saying to the inspector.

And he discovered the meaning of naked fear.

Whitley, Alan, and Louise worked most of the night. One of the spiders was almost whole, and they reckoned it must have suffocated rather than been crushed. They started on that.

"You were right about Stegodyphus," Whitley said as he put the body under a magnifying glass, "but it's no ordinary example, as you said. Let's see what he's like inside," he suggested, picking up a tray of dissecting instruments.

"Louise, could you get old hairy-legs under the microscope and I'll start chopping," Whitley smiled.

Alan had not told Peter where the spiders came from. Now he thought it was time he did.

"Peter, I don't want you to tell anyone about these insects just yet. The police are involved."

Peter looked up quickly, a puzzled look on his face.

"What are you talking about? What have the police to do with it?"

Alan noticed Louise was staring at him. He breathed in deeply and began to tell them of the deaths and of both his and the police's findings.

"Bloody hell," muttered Peter, when he had finished.

"That's exactly what Bradshaw said," Alan sighed, his face serious.

"That's . . . that's horrible," Louise said, her hands visibly shaking. "Seeing three dead here means nothing. But thousands of them . . ." her voice trailed off as she tried to picture the creatures *en masse*. She shook her head, her hair glinting copper in the light.

"Let's get down to it," Alan snapped. "We can't hang about."

Peter Whitley did the major dissecting while Alan carried out chemical analyses on the other spiders. Louise alternated between the two of them, helping where she could, making coffee and taking down any notes that were necessary.

By four in the morning the scientists had done everything they felt they could reasonably do with the limited equipment. And as they compared findings, the low tone of their voices said more about the worry they felt than anything else. Louise was aware of their deep anxiety, but tried to suppress her own nervousness.

"Starting from the head or carapace," Peter began, "the two large eyes in the center show that it's basically a hunting spider, dependent on its visual capabilities for seeing prey."

"Aren't they all like that?" Louise asked.

"No, some spiders depend on feel. They sit at the edge of a web, or sometimes in the center, and wait until something gets caught. Most hunting spiders have these two large eyes, with four or six other eyes spread around in various order depending on the species. And they use all their eyes, by the way."

Alan drummed his fingers impatiently on the edge of the table.

"OK, OK, Alan," Peter tried to smile. "I know this is old hat to you, but I'm just running through what I've found—from head to toe or biting jaws to spinnerets, if you like."

"I'm sorry, pal," Alan apologized. "I just keep wondering where in the name of God these horrors are now. Go on, go on," he said quickly.

"All right. That's the outside of the head. Now we go inside and things become . . . mm, interesting? Is that the word? Anyway, this little beauty's brain is larger than any I've seen for a spider of this size. This affects the rest of the structure, because normally the brain's small, and the rest of the front part is made up of gut, first stomach, poison glands, and so on."

He paused, and noticed Alan had stopped drumming his fingers and was peering at Peter's rough sketch.

"OK," he went on. "The brain is at least twice as large as any other spider's. . . ."

"Does that mean it's intelligent?" Louise asked.

Peter shook his head. "Not necessarily. We know they move around in packs, and you don't need intelligence to do that."

"Good point," said Alan. "In fact I'd go so far as to say that *because* it hunts in packs it has no intelligence."

"I'd go along with that," Peter agreed. "But we're looking at the facts here, not trying to work out its I.Q. As I said, the sucking stomach in the front part of the creature—spiders have two stomachs," he pointed out to Louise—"the sucking stomach is smaller than one would expect, but the poison glands are larger. The mouth and jaws are very well developed and strong, which again points to the fact that it's obviously a hunting spider."

Alan winced.

"I'm sorry, Alan," Peter said. "Your father . . ."

"Yes, yes. Go on."

"Now we come to the back. As you know, the heart of a spider is in the form of a large tube running along the top of the main part of the body or abdomen. Underneath that is the second stomach, or opisthosomal stomach, which contains the digestive glands. That is where this baby breaks every known rule. I've never seen so many digestive glands, and I've never seen such a large second stomach—again in relation to the size of the creature. The heart tube is *flattened,* making more room for the opisthosomal." He paused.

"So what do you make of that?" Alan queried.

"This specimen has adapted itself to eat more than just the tiny insects, flies and so on that spiders normally live off," Whitley claimed.

"Anything else?" Alan asked.

"There are some other differences, but they are fairly minor," Peter replied. "Sex glands, silk glands, spinnerets and so on. Oh! One more thing. This lovely's got a beautiful set of gnashers."

"What do you mean?" Alan asked.

"I mean a nice, sharp set of teeth in its mouth. Nothing unusual in spiders, I grant you. But a perfect fit upper and lower, each tooth forming a perfect triangle. Again that points to a flesh-eater. And that's all I've got to contribute now. What about the chemical side?"

Alan raised his hands.

"Nothing much on that front. The poison ducts contain some kind of nerve toxin. It's impossible to say whether the poison acts as an aid to digestion, as in most spiders, or whether it's meant to numb the victim. I'll make up a sample and send it off to Oxford for more detailed analysis. Though if the police couldn't get any information from the poison they found on my father and the other victims, I doubt if we'll score any better."

The three of them sat silently for a few minutes, disappointed that they had not discovered anything more vital but knowing that there was little more they could do. It was the futility that depressed them. It was like knowing how a nuclear bomb was made but having no control over when, or where, it was exploded.

It was Alan who snapped them out of it. "Conclusions, Peter, conclusions. Dammit, we're scientists. What has our research shown us?"

Peter looked at Alan for a few seconds before replying. He knew that Alan was now wanting talk for talk's sake. And after everything his friend had been through, Peter could not blame him.

"We've got a mutant on our hands," he replied. "A freak of nature, perhaps. How or why it happened, I don't know. Apart from Stegodyphus, I can identify characteristics of at least three other species. If you'd asked me yesterday if such a creature as this was possible, I'd have said no. A hybrid of this type just doesn't make sense in anyone's book," he concluded.

"Crazy. Just plain bloody crazy!" Alan exploded, his eyes flashing. "We've spent half the night examining something that shouldn't exist; I've seen sights that deny all current knowledge of spiders, and at the end of it all what have we got?" he asked angrily. "I'll tell you. Nothing! We know nothing about its reproductive cycle, how it kills, how it eats, whether we've got babies here or fully-grown insects. In short, we're hardly any better off than when we started. And Christ knows what the buggers are doing right now!"

"Alan, please," Louise said gently laying her hand on his. "We're all tired. You've been through a lot. We know a great deal more than when we started. There's no point in shouting at us," she added quietly.

"You're right," Alan said after a moment, looking directly into her eyes. "I'm sorry." He smiled weakly.

Peter stared down at the table they were sitting at, and in a subdued voice said, "You've got a point, Alan. And there's only one way we can get more information."

Even Louise followed the logic.

Someone, somehow, had to capture a live specimen. . . .

They returned to Alan's flat, and after a few hours' sleep, Alan called Inspector Bradshaw to report on their findings.

"Your terminology doesn't mean much to me," the policeman admitted, "but what I think you're saying is we've got a new type of spider that's equipped for eating human flesh or any other kind of warm-blooded creature, and that you want us to get you a live specimen?"

"Basically, yes."

"I wish I could oblige, Alan, but we don't know what's happened to them. And, by the way," Bradshaw added, "we've had teams of men searching the vicinities of the deaths all morning. Not one lair has been uncovered."

"Jesus! That probably means the females are carrying their egg sacs around with them," Alan said. "Has *nobody* reported any more sightings?"

"Nothing. But I'm keeping it quiet as far as the press is concerned. Though God knows how long I can do that."

"Well, if you let me know as soon as anything breaks, I'd appreciate it. If your men are worried about trapping one of the monsters, I'll do it myself," Alan offered.

"I'll be in touch the minute I get any information. Maybe they've all returned to wherever they came from and we've seen the last of them."

Alan did not comment, but told Bradshaw he would contact him when the results of the venom tests came through from Oxford.

As he put the phone down, he had the cold feeling that, far from seeing the last of them, as the inspector hoped, they had only witnessed the beginning.

One hour later, when Bradshaw called again, Alan knew his instinct had been right.

"They've been spotted!" Bradshaw yelled excitedly. "A farmer saw them in his field. They've attacked a herd of cows. Left nothing."

"Where?" Alan demanded. "Where did it happen?"

"Just outside of Leigh . . ." the inspector's voice trailed off.

"Inspector Bradshaw? Are you still there? Where are the spiders now?"

"They've disappeared again. Don't ask me how. That's your job." His voice was almost inaudible.

"What's wrong, inspector? I can hardly hear you!" Alan shouted in frustration.

"Don't you realize?" Bradshaw's voice was louder this time, but more tense. "Don't you see? They're moving north. They're heading for London!"

8

Bradshaw was right in his apprehensions about the press. They soon sniffed out the story and a few small paragraphs appeared buried in the inside pages the next day. But no one took the attack on a herd of cows very seriously. And there was no connection made with the two "murders" in Kent. As far as Fleet Street editors were concerned, rampaging spiders were in the same class as man-eating dogs.

But then the jokes stopped and the stories began hitting the front pages, when a milkman on his rounds in a quiet suburb a few miles from Sevenoaks was attacked by an army of spiders. This time there were plenty of witnesses—all willing to talk to the press, radio, and television. Each willing to embellish the story with yet another imaginary fact.

By the time the reports did appear in the national press, there were eyewitness accounts of "spiders as big as giant turtles," and one witness claimed that he had "seen the milkman's hand removed in one bite."

Though it was realized that many of these stories were highly exaggerated, two indisputable facts remained: the milkman *had* been killed by spiders; and Sevenoaks was on the main commuter line to London. These facts were enough. They formed the seeds of fear from which nationwide panic could grow.

Alan Mason traveled to Kent again, to the scene of the latest slaughter, and it was there he restated to Inspector Bradshaw the urgent need to capture a live spider.

"As I said yesterday, Alan, I wish I could help you," Bradshaw said. "But they've disappeared again. That's something I'd like you to explain. How can a bloody great mass of spiders just vanish?"

"Simple," said Alan. "Forget the stories about creatures as big as turtles. The specimens we've been examining are only a little larger than normal. Spiders usualy rest up after a hunting expedition, or even after a meal," he explained. "You've seen it yourself. A spider will sit in its web in a lighted window at night gorging itself on flies and other insects. During the day it usually hides in a crack or under a stone."

"But there are thousands of them," the inspector protested.

"Yes, and there are probably hundreds of spiders in an average-sized garden at any given moment. Yet if you look around a garden you'd be lucky to spot even one."

"So?"

"So what I'm saying is this: if the spiders went off into a wood, or even an old barn, do you know how many could sleep there, remaining perfectly still, without you knowing it?"

Bradshaw nodded. "Of course."

"Well, then. You imagine a hayloft covered from floor to ceiling with spiders. Given their size, you could get hundreds of thousands in a relatively small space."

"So if we found where they rested, could we wipe them out?"

"Possibly, but I doubt it. There could be more than one pack. As I say, think how many could rest in one good-sized oak tree and you begin to realize the dimension of the problem."

"We can't do anything about them," Bradshaw said desperately. "The manpower alone needed to comb an area after they've appeared again would be immense. And, as you say, even then hundreds of them could be missed. What the hell's going to happen?"

"I don't know, inspector. I honestly don't know."

Nothing in fact happened for two days. There were no reports of sightings, no cases of animals or people suddenly disappearing. The papers moved on to more current and important news, such as the rising price of tea and coffee.

Alan received a more accurate breakdown of the spider's venom from the Oxford labs. Again, it was basically similar to normal poison, but with marked differences. Made up of various protein components, the scientists had injected it into a series of animals to discover the poison's effects.

Every warm-blooded animal was affected identically. At first no immediate reaction, then drowsiness followed by a hideous distortion of the area where the venom was introduced. It seemed as if the venom had the ability to destroy the lymphocytes in the body, the cells which fought disease. But it also created mutant, monster cells which multiplied rapidly, causing huge swellings. Left alone, these mutant cells made their way to the brain, which in turn would begin to swell and press against the skull until it literally burst.

No poison like it had been known in medical history. And, because of this, no existing antidote would be effective.

Alan called Bradshaw with the news. The inspector sounded tired.

"Great news, Alan," he said sarcastically. "Not only can't we find them, but if they attack and bite, then we've had it anyway. Terrific."

Alan remained silent. The inspector was only voicing his own fearful thoughts.

"No more news of them, I suppose?"

"Nothing. And *that's* driving me crazy as well."

"Don't forget to call me as soon as anything happens. We need some of them alive," Alan reminded him and hung up.

Any false sense of security was shattered with horrifying suddenness.

A primary school to the north of Sevenoaks was swamped with spiders late in the afternoon. Most of the children luckily managed to escape, but a few had been bitten. The total death toll was thirty-four, including two teachers.

The waiting game was over, and everyone, especially the inhabitants of London, now sat up and took notice. As the reports on the children in the hospital leaked out, describing their slow, agonizing death, a nervousness began to spread among the public.

An Action Team was set up, including Bradshaw and Alan among its members, along with some top Government scientists and civil servants. No one was treating the spiders lightly any longer.

"We've at least got an idea of their direction," Alan said to Bradshaw as they stood outside the deserted school the next day. "My guess is that they're still moving north, and we should be able to trace a bunch of them if we look carefully."

Bradshaw agreed and put twenty men on search duty. It was not long before a call came through saying that hundreds of spiders had been observed going into a disused garage about two miles north of the afflicted school.

"All right," ordered Bradshaw, all tiredness gone, "let's move."

"Have you got all the gear I asked for?" Alan asked.

"Waiting in the Range Rover," Bradshaw replied, already moving toward the white car.

On the way the two men changed into fire-fighting suits which completely covered their bodies. The material was a thick silvery plastic, and they put hoods with clear visors over their heads. Thick gloves completed the outfit, and Alan hoped it would be sufficient protection against the spiders' claws and biting jaws.

They reached the garage a few minutes later. Two police vans were waiting at a safe distance. It was one o'clock and the garage, standing beside the deserted ruins of a house, looked peaceful. Fields stretched all around it; the black earth was bare, the harvest having just been collected. Under normal circumstances it would have been a perfect rural scene.

Two policemen also changed into protective suits. Then Alan picked up a cylinder filled with pressurized ether. Bradshaw and the policemen carried flamethrowers.

The four men approached the building slowly. Nothing stirred and Alan became acutely aware of the silence around them. With sickening insight he realized that the spiders had probably eaten all the birds and other wildlife in the area.

They paused at the entrance of the garage. One crumbling wooden door hung open on rusty hinges. Alan peered in before taking a step forward. It was dark, and he noticed old, dusty cobwebs at the entrance. Obviously not those of the killer spiders, he thought. He indicated by sign language that the men get busy with the flamethrowers as soon as he made a move.

Alan darted into the garage. At first the gloom prevented him from seeing anything, but soon his eyes adjusted and he looked around.

All four walls and the ceiling were alive with the spiders. A black mass poured down the walls toward the garage entrance, at which Bradshaw and the others now directed wide arcs of flame. The march of spiders halted, wavered, turned back. Alan felt thudding bodies fall on him from the roof as more spiders swung down on silk strands. His visor was covered with frantic, struggling insects.

Brushing them off with his gloved hand, he aimed the ether at the ground in front of him. The whole floor seemed to heave with life. As he stepped forward, Alan felt tiny bodies crunch beneath his boots.

By the light of the flamethrowers, he shuddered to see dozens of the creatures clinging to his suit, trying to bite their way through the thick material. Ignoring them, he concentrated on directing the fine whitish spray from the nozzle gripped in his hand.

And, then, in the hellish red glare he observed four large black shapes crawling slowly over the other, smaller spiders toward him. At first he could not, would not, believe that they, too, were spiders. But as they advanced nearer there was no mistaking the rounded hair-covered body, the back half raised, and the front multi-eyed section swaying slowly from side to side as each creature's eight legs rose and fell in awful symmetry.

They halted facing Alan and, as one, the four giants raised their front pairs of legs in the air, swinging them from side to side. Alan shuddered as he watched this grisly ritual, and sweat poured off his forehead. The sweat of fear.

The large biting jaws began to open and close as the giants continued their nightmare advance toward him. Fighting the panicky urge to run, Alan trained the nozzle of the ether gun on the leading spider. He pressed the release button. The spider did not stop its silent march.

Lowering the nozzle until it was only a foot from the creature, Alan opened the control valve on the cylinder to FULL.

Suddenly the horror before him was shrouded in mist and, when Alan lifted the gun, he saw the creature was still, its legs curled beneath it. The other three were nowhere to be seen. Unclipping a thick polythene bag from his belt, he placed the creature into it and snapped the neck of the bag tightly shut.

This action drove the smaller spiders wild. They

turned on the other men and clambered over the fire suits, desperately trying to find a chink in the protective armor.

Alan gestured with his hand and the four men retreated slowly backward toward the entrance. The flamethrowers spat out instant death to scores of insects —but it was as if there was no end to them.

Alan turned to run—but stopped when he saw the other three giant spiders now standing in a line between him and the garage entrance. He feared that their biting jaws would be able to cut through his fire-suit, and when the spiders started to edge back towards him he felt there was no chance for him.

One of the policemen, spotting the giants for the first time, instinctively aimed his flamethrower at them and switched on. Nothing happened. The man shook the tube violently. Still nothing. Bradshaw and the other policemen were concentrating on spraying flame over the hordes of smaller spiders all around them and did not notice. Alan, realizing the flamethrower had jammed, looked wildly around for another escape route. There was none.

And then in horror he watched the policeman tuck the flamethrower under one arm and take his glove off to adjust it.

"Keep your gloves on, for God's sake, man!" he yelled. "Don't be bloody stupid!" But it was useless. He could not be heard through his visor, never mind the surrounding commotion.

Alan stood helpless as he saw half a dozen spiders drop from the man's hood on to his exposed hand, biting viciously through the skin. The policeman dropped the flamethrower and tried to shake the insects off. They clung like leeches.

The three large spiders had now stopped, sensing the proximity of blood and flesh. Rounding on the unfortunate policeman—pulling their fat, heavy bodies along with incredible speed—they reached him within seconds, front legs poised in the air, biting jaws and poison fangs at the ready.

Alan had been right. He shuddered as he watched the giant spiders cut through the fireproof material as easily as through dry parchment.

Their victim fell and the giants began tearing at his legs, soon exposing the flesh. Smaller spiders greedily swarmed on to the open wounds, ripping segments of bloodied skin away from his calves.

Bradshaw and the other policemen stood by, flame-throwers in hand, unable to help, frightened of scorching the ravaged policeman on the floor.

Alan, feeling violently sick, ran out through the garage door and toward the waiting cars. A few minutes later Bradshaw and the other men stumbled way from the garage as it flared up, long flames licking into the air, black smoke billowing everywhere.

Alan yanked his hood away as the men reached them.

"What . . . happened?" he stammered.

Bradshaw pulled his visor off. He was white-faced.

"We burned him. You should have seen his eyes behind the visor as those bastards ate him. We had no choice. We burned him," he repeated.

There was silence as the group of men watched their chief duck behind the Range Rover. Only the crackling sound of the burning garage could be heard in the still air . . . and the violent retching of Inspector Bradshaw.

9

Charlie, as Alan had nicknamed the giant spider—his macabre trophy—gazed malevolently out of its cage. Its eight eyes stared unblinkingly ahead, focused on Alan's back as he stooped over a bench in the lab. Louise was also in the room, and an Indian doctor, Naren Patim, an expert on toxicology—the study of poisons.

All three looked very tired. They had been working almost nonstop for forty-eight hours, trying to find an antidote for the spider venom. With no success. Peter Whitley came in with a tray of coffees. He had been working with the others, and the lines of disappointment on his face reflected everyone's feelings.

For now it was a race against time. From the smaller spiders Alan had bagged, they had discovered that the female did in fact carry its egg sac around with it. And, worse, each sac contained nearly four hundred eggs.

When they had definitely established its method of reproduction, there was no hiding their fear. Peter calculated that if the spiders bred normally it would be only a matter of three months before the whole of southeast England was totally covered with the gruesome creatures.

This information had been instantly passed to the Prime Minister, who, for obvious reasons, kept it from the press. But the public was beginning to panic. The spiders, now advancing rapidly on London, were striking at any time of day. This was another aberration, Whitley pointed out, since the insects normally hunted at night.

Every living thing in the spiders' path was destroyed.

Cows, sheep, farm animals, stables full of horses, were wiped out, and the countryside from mid Kent to the outskirts of London was soon devoid of any bird life. A deathly silence followed in the wake of the spiders' progress.

People in the Farnborough, Orpington, Croydon, and Bromley areas were attacked in their homes. Those escaping with only bites soon died anyway, their bodies swollen and bloated beyond recognition.

A trainload of commuters from Sevenoaks destined for Charing Cross was set upon one clear and bracing morning. The driver was the first bitten and then devoured, and as the train careened onward out of control his murderers rampaged through the carriages. When the train crashed and turned over, the passengers were spilled out like broken dolls. As they lay there, bleeding and weeping, the spiders scuttled among them with deadly purpose, biting, tearing, destroying.

Fear was building up throughout the capital, and the Government issued an official statement asking people not to leave, claiming everything was under control. No one believed this, of course. The creatures were advancing and it seemed as if nothing could effectively stop them.

As panic grew, everything became suspect, and in this lay the worst horror. Any slight movement was instantly noticed. Every gutter, every tree, every bush— anything that possibly could hide a spider became an object of fear. Men, women, and children became too terrified to walk through the London streets in case a stream of spiders should pour up suddenly through the drains.

People who lived near parks or had trees in their gardens lived now in constant terror. Leaves blown along by the wind became the enemy to fevered, fear-filled minds.

Even inhabitants of high-rise buildings could get no

peace. Elevator shafts represented cages of death after spiders had entered an office block in Croydon and, swarming through the building, had short-circuited the electrical system. An elevator full of people going home had been stuck halfway down the shaft. The safety hatch at the top had been opened—only to let in a deluge of murderous insects, which dropped through the open space on top of the screaming, struggling, hysterical group of trapped victims.

When police finally managed to get the elevator down, there was nothing in it but skeletal figures, most of them crowded in one corner in an attempt to escape their inevitable, horrifying death.

Mothers kept children from school; men sealed their houses as best they could with polythene over all windows and openings; the streets of London were deserted after nightfall; the restaurants, theaters, and cinemas closed down.

London was going mad.

And the spiders were seen on Blackheath, ten miles from the center of the capital.

The army was sent out to the large, flat green space. The spiders danced their grisly dance across Blackheath, the "giants," as they were now called, in the center. Gas, flames, bullets, and chemicals were projected at the creatures in an attempt to stop their onward march. But the spiders merely split into groups and poured into the deserted buildings on either side of the Heath, into the thousands of hiding places that the empty houses, gardens, garages, and warehouses offered them.

This produced a state of deadlock—and chaos reigned. London resembled a wartorn city. Escaping cars jammed the M1 and all routes north. Heathrow was closed down, and all planes were diverted to Manchester. The police no longer attempted to control the maddened crowds struggling to leave the city. Basic services, telephones, and electricity rapidly began to deteriorate. The royal family was flown to Canada—a final signal of despair for the public, who soon discovered the fact despite attempts to hush it up.

Many doctors and nurses stuck to their posts as long as possible, but the hospitals were soon overflowing with the screaming, tortured, blown-up victims of spider bites.

It was becoming clear to everyone, particularly to the Government, that there seemed no way of stopping the carnage.

Alan Mason and the Action Team stayed in London, working round the clock to find an answer to the crisis. There seemed none, and the best they could hope for was to discover an antidote to the venom. Alan, like the others, was living on his nerves, always conscious of the fact that even the smallest crack in a wall, the tiniest space under a door, was a potential entrance for spiders.

Sleep was almost impossible; for Alan, like the rest of the population of London, the dark took on new terrors, and the closing of eyes could mean missing a telltale movement in the shadows.

It was only a matter of time before everything finally broke down.

"We're moving you out of here. Get your stuff together and be ready by 11 A.M. tomorrow, please."

Alan stared at Sir Stanley Jenson, the senior civil servant who was one of the Action Committee, the administrative unit of the Action Team. He did not particularly like Jenson, and was constantly annoyed by the man's insistence on sticking rigidly to the rules, despite the circumstances.

"What the hell for?" Alan asked. "We've got everything we need here."

"The Prime Minister, acting on advice, feels that

you would be safer in a building in North London. Staying here, right beside the river, is asking for trouble."

"Why's that? I thought the theory was that the spiders wouldn't be able to cross the Thames," Alan insisted. "What was the point of blocking the Blackwall and Dartford Tunnels? Why are there armed soldiers on every bleeding bridge that crosses the river? We're working well here. We don't need disruption. No, and I'm sure I'm speaking for everyone, you can stuff your recommendation."

Sir Stanley Jenson quivered. Alan had never seen anyone quivering, and smiled, trying hard not to burst out laughing. It was a ridiculous sight. The civil servant's nostrils widened and closed rapidly. His face had gone red and his hands were visibly shaking. Alan found himself loving every second of it.

Eventually Sir Stanley calmed down.

"I suppose you don't *read* the daily bulletin you receive every morning from the AC?" With an army background, Sir Stanley converted everything to initials, including the Action Committee.

"I never look at them," Alan confessed. "Too busy. And now . . ."

"Then obviously you haven't read this morning's news," Sir Stanley interrupted.

Alan shook his head, fearing he was about to hear another new rule devised by the civil servants.

"Despite our attempts to contain the spiders, they've managed to cross the Thames."

"How? And where?" Alan retorted, all humor gone from his voice.

"We think, but we're not certain, that they got across somewhere near Gravesend."

"They can't swim. They'd be drowned," Alan protested.

"It seems there's a point, when the tide is out, where

it's possible to cross on almost dry land. They had a whole night to get over."

"Jesus," Alan sighed and his body sagged with weariness at the futility of it all. "We're finished."

"It didn't really make much difference," Jenson went on, his voice calm now. "You see—and this isn't generally known—the spiders were sweeping across to Hampshire and around toward London anyway. The fact that they crossed the river at Gravesend means nothing. They would have reached North London from the west, anyway."

"That means they're spreading across the whole country."

"Exactly, Mason. Now, if you could arrange your equipment, please."

Alan nodded.

"We'll be ready," he said flatly, wondering what good it would do.

The next day they moved into a modern glass building four stories high in North London. It had previously been owned by a chemical manufacturing company, and Alan had to admit that it was a good choice. With soldiers on duty around the clock, and every facility the scientists needed, they could work there in peace—and manage to have some sleep. They moved the captured spiders in too, Charlie being given pride of place near the window.

Reports had come in all day of the spiders' advance over the country. London was so fast becoming a ghost city that there were few cases of human mortality.

Bert Jackson poured himself a large mug of tea. This was the time of night he enjoyed most. The animals were nicely settled; he could relax in his office with his feet up and watch whatever television was still transmitted. Peace reigned over the Andover Dogs' Home. Just the way Bert liked it.

He turned on the television set, twisting the tuning dial. He caught the end of some late night news, before the station went off the air. Disappointed, he picked up a book, a cheap Western, and was soon immersed in it.

Just after midnight he went to put the kettle on for another cup of tea. He was about to light the gas ring when he heard a dog bark. And then another. And another.

"What the bloody hell . . ." he swore as he put down the kettle.

By the time he had reached the end of the long corridor which led to the cages, it seemed to him that every animal in the building was barking and howling. They were not normal sounds, but long, wailing cries of fear.

Opening the door of the main section, he was met with a bedlam of deafening sound. Flicking on the light switch Bert peered down the rows of cages. At first all he could see were maddened dogs flinging themselves against the bars, yelping, barking, and howling.

And then he saw them. The spiders. They were through the cages, attacking the trapped animals. A movement on the far wall showed Bert how the creatures had entered. High on the wall a small ventilation window had been left open. A steady stream poured through it.

"Oh God," he sobbed. "Oh dear God." He loved his animals.

Bert looked desperately around, but there was nothing he could do. He gazed aghast as one large Alsatian, its head and stomach black with biting insects, gnawed desperately at the iron bars of its prison, froth mingled with blood pouring from its lacerated mouth.

In the next cage a mongrel lay on its side, its body ripped open and the intestines seeping out onto the floor. Bert retched at the sight of the spiders crawling in and out of its stomach.

Every cage he could see told a similar story. It was a massacre. The animals had no chance.

Bert stepped back slowly and slammed the door closed behind him. He ran to his office and phoned the police. By the time they arrived to comfort the weeping Bert, peace reigned over Andover Dogs' Home once again.

Occasional stories came in from Kent, Surrey, and Hampshire of entire families wiped out. Farming families mainly, too proud to leave the land. Or a hippy community who believed that God would spare them—they were completely annihilated.

And then one day the killings stopped.

No reports were received the next day either. Not one person or animal had been attacked. No sightings were made and no new areas were pronounced spider-infested.

The creatures had simply disappeared from the face of the earth.

The authorities at first held back the news, not wanting to raise false hopes. But when there was no change the next day, they decided to issue a statement.

Not a spider was seen for a week, two weeks, and then a month. Human nature being what it is, the population of London and the surrounding country drifted slowly, then rapidly, back from the emergency camps that had been set up in the Midlands. A semblance of normal life began to return to the capital. A few restaurants reopened; even some theaters began to play again.

At first newspapers, radio, and television devoted whole pages and programs to theorizing on what had happened to the creatures. But gradually normal world events took over the front pages again.

Nearly everyone was convinced that the danger had passed. But not Alan Mason.

10

"I don't think they've gone," Alan told Inspector Bradshaw firmly. "There were too many of them. And there was nothing in their way. Whatever happened, I don't think we've seen the last of them."

"Nothing has been seen for nearly a month. Even if they were breeding, food would be needed for the young, wouldn't it?"

Alan shook his head.

"No. There are certain species of spider where the newly-hatched young feed off the female, which dies as soon as the eggs are hatched. Our type could be one of these."

The two men were in Alan's flat. They had continued seeing each other even after the Action Team had been disbanded the previous week.

"Well, Mr. Know-it-all Mason," Bradshaw joked. "Have *you* got a theory about what's happened?"

Alan looked sternly at the inspector, but with a twinkle in his eyes. "Yes, I've got a theory."

"Well, let's hear it then," the inspector grimaced.

Louise came in from the kitchen carrying a tray with three coffees and some biscuits. She was smiling, and with her hair reflected in the light behind her, she looked radiant.

Since the trouble had started, she had hardly left Alan's side. Which was the way he liked it. Her amazing capacity for work, her constant good humor, and her unquestioning approach to nearly everything had increased his love and respect for her daily. Now Alan could not imagine living without her, and she had moved into his apartment on their return from the Action Team labs in North London. Every morning, when he awoke, he thrilled to see her lying beside him, a naked arm flung carelessly across the blanket, her full lips moving slightly in her sleep as she dreamed.

Gently touching her, he would wake her, and then, both still sleep-warm, they would make slow, deliberate love. For Alan each lovemaking session was different, a new experience, and often, as they sat in the apartment reading or working, he would pause and look at her, appreciating the lines of her face, her green laughing eyes, and soft hair.

In short, he was deeply in love with the lady.

That was what he was thinking now as he watched her set down the coffee cups, and he winked at her when she handed him his.

"Well, then, let's hear this theory of yours," Bradshaw insisted. "How come, in the face of all evidence, you think the little beasts are still around."

"Simple," Alan began. "Apart from following their breeding instincts, the spiders are resting up, growing stronger . . ."

"How can they grow stronger without food?"

"That's exactly it. Don't forget we're dealing with a hybrid, a combination of different types of spider. Even though it varies in size. It's known that certain spiders can exist for up to thirty days without food, living off the reserve of fat stored in their bodies. And because these horrors have been *eating* fat, there's no telling how long they can go without needing food."

Bradshaw was silent as he looked long and hard at Alan.

"Let's hope to God you're wrong," he commented finally, his voice heavy with concern.

The following morning, Sunday, Alan and Louise lay in bed enjoying the breakfast he had cooked.

"Not bad," Louise said between mouthfuls of bacon and egg. "You'll make someone a good wife one day."

"Hmmm. Could do at that," he said.

"Mind you, I don't think you'd be much good at housekeeping. If it wasn't for me, this place would be a real pigsty," she smiled.

"Are you implying I'm a pig?"

"I'm not *implying* anything, my darling. I'm stating it outright."

"Put that tray on the floor," Alan demanded.

Louise laid the tray down, knowing what was coming. Alan lunged across the bed and grappled her playfully, his hands tickling her between the legs, his mouth exploring her naked body.

"If I'm an animal, then I'll behave like one," he said. "Any complaints?"

She took his head between her palms and kissed him. She felt his hands stop their rough progress over her body and settle gently over the front of her breasts, making circular motions around her nipples.

She moaned and abandoned herself to his attentions. Using mouth and fingers expertly, he brought her to orgasm even before entering her. And when he did move on top, slowly easing himself into her, she felt tears rolling down her cheeks. Tears of happiness, tears of confirmation that for them making love was not a release from frustration but a positive statement. . . .

That afternoon, they visited Alan's mother, now gradually recovering from her bereavement. And on their way home, the couple called in at Peter Whitley's home. Peter shared Alan's continuing concern about the spiders and he, too, believed it would only be a matter of time before they surfaced again. Naturally they discussed the creatures.

"Are the city workers still refusing to go down to the sewers?" he asked Alan.

Despite Government and Council assurances, sewage

workers had threatened strike action rather than go underground until *they* were convinced all the spiders were gone. And for that they wanted visible proof.

"As far as I know, they are," Alan replied. "But the spiders could be anywhere, not just down the sewers. The useless Government!" he spat. "I advised them to put every available man on the job of searching for the mutants. But no, they said, if there were no sightings, no killings, then why should they spend fortunes of public money looking for something that wasn't there."

Peter shook his head. "You're right. Do you know that cretin Sir Stanley Jenson actually told me that the whole thing had been a freak of Nature, and Nature herself had taken care of the problem?" he said angrily. "Blind. That's what they are, criminally blind."

"Now, now, gentlemen," Louise said with a smile. "Calm down. At least if the spiders do reappear, we've got an antidote against their bites. They won't be able to cause as many deaths."

Alan and Peter, with Naren Patim, had continued working on the venom even after it was announced that the immediate danger was over. They felt the lull, if that was what it was, gave them a chance to work without pressure. Within a few days the first hopeful signs came through and soon the men had developed a satisfactory antidote to the bizarre poison.

It was a discovery that a few weeks before would have brought them the thanks of the nation, the congratulations of the Government, and their entry into the history books. But with the spiders apparently gone, they received only mild official thanks for their work, a two-paragraph mention in *The Times,* and their cure was filed away for future reference.

The Reverend Frederick J. Bodley, Church of England, Hampstead, stood smiling and nodding as he greeted the congregation entering his church. It was a clear day, though a bank of clouds to the west threatened rain. The clock struck ten and the minister turned back into the body of the church. It was a gratifying sight for a man of the cloth. Nearly all the seats were filled. If only it could be like this every Sunday, Reverend Bodley thought.

It had been the Archbishop's idea in the first place. A national day of thanksgiving to the Lord for delivery from the spiders. The Roman Catholic bishops had taken up the idea as well. The Queen and the royal family would attend a special service in Westminster Abbey.

As the Reverend Bodley closed the thick oak doors behind him, and walked down the nave past crowded pews, he wondered if the spiders had been sent by the Lord in the first place, to make people turn back to the truth of the church.

A squat, heavy-jowled man in his mid-fifties, Bodley had a constantly sympathetic look about him. A trustworthy look. And as he approached the altar that Sunday morning his brown eyes shone with the joy that only true faith brought.

He looked around the church. Men, women, and children gazed at him expectantly. Families were there who had not seen the inside of a church since the previous Christmas—if at all. It was indeed a gratifying and inspiring sight for the good Reverend.

He glanced up at the small gallery. The organist, Bob Riley, sat ready before the large reed organ whose pipes stretched up to the roof.

Bodley commenced by reminding the congregation why they were there. He quoted Acts, Chapter 12, the salvation of Peter. He grasped the edge of the altar and his voice thundered through the nave when he came to the verse about the word of God growing and multiplying. A baby had begun to cry, but Bodley, now in full swing, with the congregation hanging on every word, asked if the spiders were not like one of the ten plagues sent by the Lord against the heathen Pharaoh. The congregation nodded silently. It was a moving moment.

The Reverend motioned to the organist, who began to quietly play.

"We shall sing Psalm 20, a psalm of salvation and deliverance," Bodley intoned, and waited until the congregation had turned to the relevant page.

Bob Riley concentrated on the sheet music propped up in front of him. The music swelled through the church and the congregation sang loud and clear. Humming along with the tune, Riley did not perceive a black shape dart out from one of the organ pipes and scuttle toward his hand. Nor did he see the shadowy movements issuing from behind the taller pipes beyond, or the seething commotion starting on the spandreled roof.

The first spider moved quickly across the shiny mahogany surface, its eyes watching Riley's fingers flit over the keys. Then it darted forward, its biting jaws at the ready, and sank them into the back of his left hand.

Riley jumped back over his stool.

"No, no. Oh, my God, no," he shouted, as the music tailed off eerily. But his cries were unheard over the heartfelt singing.

He flicked his hand violently until the spider fell off. About to run, he froze, his voice choked with fear, when he saw a solid shadow of spiders spill from the pipes and over the organ toward him.

Within seconds they had covered his body. Thrashing his arms wildly, he stepped back to the edge of the gallery. Desperately clawing at his eyes, he toppled over the railing and crashed down on to the startled congregation.

When the music had stopped, Reverend Bodley looked up at the gallery, but could only barely make out Riley's frantic movements. Then the organist moved back, and he could see the spiders crawling over the crazed man's body. Bodley panicked.

"The doors! The doors! Get to the doors!" he yelled.

But it was too late. Down from the high roof thousands of spiders were falling as fast as unholy rain.

Bodley stood helpless above the struggling, fighting, screaming crowd. He watched as a mother grabbed her two young children and tried to run for the doors, only to disappear under a heap of grasping, punching, and kicking bodies . . . and a deadly mantle of poisonous insects.

Only a few congregants managed to get to the doors and fling them open, spiders clinging to their bodies as they rushed into the street. Bodley turned away and knelt before the huge cross with a representation of the crucified Christ upon it. Clasping his hands, he raised his eyes, now glazed with terror and disbelief, toward the Christ's face.

His mind did not register the black shapes moving swiftly over the sculpture and its bleeding feet. Bodley repeated passages from the Lord's Prayer over and over. He did not move when the first spiders clambered over his smock and reached his hands, biting and tearing. Only when one spider bit deep into his jugular vein did he finally react. Falling forward he unclasped his hands and stretched them out toward the cross. This made him all the more vulnerable to his oppressors, who rapidly finished their work of destruction.

The carnage was over in less than ten minutes. Finally only quiet moans and an occasional sob could be heard. Then silence. Like smoke drifting across a wasteland the spiders moved silently out of the church, through the graveyard, and toward the safety of Hampstead Heath with its trees, bushes, and long grass.

The spiders had returned.

The phone was ringing in Alan's flat when they arrived home. It was Bradshaw.

"You were right," he said wearily. "They're back. Thousands of them. We've got eighty deaths already on our hands."

Alan felt weak, and slumped down in a chair beside the phone.

"Where?"

"Hampstead. In a church. The congregation didn't have a chance. Can you get over there?"

"Of course," Alan muttered.

Fifteen minutes later the two men stood together outside a church off Hampstead Hill, watching dozens of stretchers, each covered by a white sheet, being carried out to the scores of waiting ambulances.

"How did it happen?" Alan asked the policeman.

"From what we can gather from the one or two people still alive, the congregation was caught completely unawares," he said. "As you can see there's only one entrance at the front, and that was closed. It looks as if the spiders were in the roof and the belfry tower up there."

Alan glanced at the high tower, and nodded slowly.

"There could easily have been thousands of them in that," he sighed.

". . . with nowhere to run," Bradshaw went on in a flat, toneless voice, ignoring Alan's comment; "they never had a hope. . . . Men, women, and children. I've been in there, and I don't want to see anything like it again."

This time the panic was worse. Totally uncontrolled mobs of hopeless people ignored pleas for calm and headed out of London. After the previous assurances that everything had been done to eliminate the spiders, no one was ready to believe the authorities again. Policemen regularly clashed with angry mobs and there were several deaths.

But worse, much worse, a slow realization spread, like the roots of a tree, that there was *nowhere* to go that was safe. With spiders infesting the southeast, as far west as Salisbury, and beginning to appear in Berkshire, Buckinghamshire, and East Anglia, what part of Britain was safe? It looked as if most of its population was doomed.

So, despite the plans being made for the evacuation of London, even the authorities had to admit that it was a pointless exercise in the long term.

Where, they asked, *can the people go?*

11

The air in the small room was blue with smoke. Alan watched as men shouted at each other, waved their fists in the air, thumped on the long table around which they sat.

The Action Committee and Team were in a conference room at the Ministry of the Environment building, the irony of which had not escaped Alan and Neil Bradshaw who sat next to each other, sickened by the childish display in front of them.

"And these are the people who run the country," Bradshaw whispered, shaking his head.

Alan stared grimly ahead, eyes hooded and teeth clenched.

Sir Stanley Jenson banged on the table with a small ashtray.

"Gentlemen, please! Some order! We're getting as bad as the mobs outside!" he yelled. "I've just come from the Prime Minister, who has given us authority, subject to his approval, to take any measures necessary to put an end to the onslaught of the spiders. Can we hear your suggestions, please."

General George Harper, the man responsible for deploying the Army in this emergency, had a simple solution.

"We could blow the bastards up," he said. "We've got enough armaments to wipe them off the face of the earth. Once we've gone in with bombs, incendiary devices, and maybe . . ." he paused, unsure if he should carry on.

"Nuclear weapons?" someone finished the sentence for him.

"If necessary, yes," the general said. "If normal methods won't work, we have no alternative."

The committee was silent. While it was true that the crisis had grown over the last month, the prospect of exploding even the smallest nuclear bomb held the risk of unleashing a still greater hell.

"Any other suggestions?" Sir Stanley asked coldly.

"I see no reason why we can't spray London and the whole surrounding area with a killer gas—up to a radius of fifty miles, perhaps," proposed Charles Pollock, a biochemist.

"What kind of gas do you have in mind?" Alan asked.

"A type that destroys cells. We've got one, you know."

"No doubt," Alan commented cynically. "But this gas would destroy *all* living cells, wouldn't it?"

Pollock nodded enthusiastically. "Without question," he said.

"Including all plants, and grass?"

Pollock nodded, and this time more slowly.

"And the millions of termites and other small insects that feed the earth?"

Pollock reluctantly agreed.

"Then I don't think that's a feasible proposition, do you?" Alan concluded. "What you're actually saying is that we should destroy six and a half thousand square miles of Britain, leaving land that wouldn't be workable for decades."

There were murmurs of concern from around the table.

"But with the spiders there now, the land is already useless," Pollock insisted, unwilling to see his plan so easily dismissed.

"Quite true," General Harper commented.

"I agree," Alan nodded. "But look at it this way. Can you be certain that you'll kill *all* of the spiders?

Where do you draw the line? You said fifty miles. OK. What if some spiders then turn up seventy-five miles from London? You spray a wider circle. And then what? More spiders a hundred miles from London. I don't think I have to go on, gentlemen. Remember how they breed. The only way a killer spray is going to ensure total destruction of all the spiders is for us to cover the whole of Britain with the gas. By killing literally every living cell in England, Scotland, and Wales. It's the only hope of wiping them out that way," he emphasized. "And the same applies to General Harper's suggestion. There's no guarantee that you'll wipe them all out without having to turn the whole of Britain into a nuclear wasteland."

No one moved. Sir Stanley stared at Alan, his face white and drawn. In a quiet and subdued voice he asked for further alternatives.

"What about poisoning them?" someone suggested.

Sir Stanley looked questioningly at Alan, who was shaking his head.

"Spiders eat only live food," Alan said wearily, running his hand through his hair. "And the poison needed to kill them off would also kill outright any animals injected with it before the spiders ever got a chance to attack them. They won't touch carcasses. If we could corner them in a quarry, with no means of escape, they would even eat each other," he pointed out. "But that, of course, is impossible, because of their sheer numbers."

Two more suggestions came up and were flung out. The first was to set parts of London on fire. That was immediately rejected because it would only drive the creatures out of the capital into the country.

The second suggestion was met with even more derision. "Dam up the Thame and flood London," someone said.

"You'd be lucky to kill a thousand spiders that

way," Alan claimed. "And with the number of skyscrapers in central London—where the flooding would be worst—they would just keep climbing and wait for the waters to subside."

When Sir Stanley again asked for suggested solutions there was a long silence. Finally he turned to Alan.

"Mason," he began. "You've pointed out the flaws in all the proposals put forward so far, but do you yourself have any idea how we can wipe out this menace?"

"None at all," Alan admitted. "I only wish I had."

Thus the meeting ended.

Alan returned to the labs reopened in the north of London and read the latest bulletins on the spider invasion.

"God damn it!" he spat, glaring at Charlie, the giant spider which stared back at him from its cage. Charlie and its smaller co-prisoners had been kept alive for further experiments. The cage, all glass reinforced with wire mesh, had a long, thick pipe sprouting from one corner, through which live mice and rats were dropped to feed the hellish creature within.

Alan waved the bulletins angrily at the cage.

"What the hell are you?" he shouted. "Where did you come from?"

He went across and banged the top of the cage. Charlie scurried around in the confined space, trying to find means of escape. The bulletins were not good news. It was now apparent that the spiders were breeding faster and becoming hungrier. According to the reports there was scarcely an animal or bird left alive within a ten-mile radius of Greater London.

Alan gazed down at Charlie. Even after weeks of working with it and the other spiders, he still had a feeling of revulsion whenever he looked at the giant. Its huge body was joined in the center to a short, thick neck, and the eight stocky legs, covered with bristles, moved as silently as death.

But it was Charlie's eyes that struck a chord of fear in Alan as old as civilization itself. The two large eyes in the center of the black, hair-covered visage, and the six others around it. They constantly stared—cold, glassy, and emotionless. Dead eyes.

He watched the spider pad noiselessly around the bottom of the cage, and again brought his fist down with a bang on the top.

"You bastard! You've got us, haven't you?" he raved. "Christ, I wish I knew what caused you! How you started . . ." his voice trailed off—and then the shadow of a smile began to play around his lips.

He rushed across to a large-scale map of southeast England stuck on one wall. Red pins marked the sites of all the known spider attacks, and they stretched across the map in mad profusion. But, Alan realized excitedly, there *was* a pattern.

He called Inspector Bradshaw.

"Look, it may not be much—if anything—but I think I'm now on to something," he almost shouted down the phone. "Can you get across here quickly?"

Bradshaw reached the labs twenty minutes later. Alan showed him the map.

"Look at these pins, Neil," he said. "Can you see anything?"

"Pins. That's all. Just pins," the inspector answered, perplexed at the question.

"Yes, yes. Of course," Alan retorted irritably. "But there's a pattern to them. They move out from this one point—in fact from the old farmhouse that my parents bought. Look here. All the deaths started in that small area."

Bradshaw stared at Alan puzzled.

"You mean you called me out here to tell me *that*?" he queried. "Of course the plague, or whatever you want to call it, first showed itself at Dragon's Farm. We all know that. It's obvious. . . ."

"I know it's obvious!" Alan interrupted, clenching his fists in exasperation. "And maybe because it is so bloody obvious we've all missed it!"

Bradshaw laid a hand on Alan's arm.

"Alan, please slow down. I don't know what you're talking about. Can you start again."

Alan ran his fingers through his hair and sighed.

"Neil, don't you see? The spiders had to start *somewhere*. If we can find the precise spot, we may discover what *caused* them to be the freaks they are. That somewhere must be near Dragon's Farm!"

Bradshaw frowned in thought. It *was* obvious.

"So what do we do now?" he asked quickly, caught up in Alan's fever-pitch excitement.

"Get out all the records of the district for the last . . . say, fifty years. And try to get in touch with some of the people who lived down there. Can you do that?"

"Damn right I can!" Bradshaw said, walking across to the phone. "This is right up my alley. And we've got something positive to work on at last."

"Hang on, hang on," Alan said. "When you find the records, look for *anything* unusual."

"Like what?"

"Peter Whitley once suggested the spiders may have come from abroad. See if anyone there received imported bananas or other fruits in packing cases. Or even foreign machinery," he added.

"And what do you want to know from the folk who used to live in the farmhouse?"

"Same thing. Any odd event. Inexplicable illnesses among the sheep or cows. It's good farming country down in that part of Kent. Someone must have noticed something."

Bradhsaw had a dozen men searching the county records within half an hour, and another dozen tracing the whereabouts of the previous tenants. Radio and television announcements were made every hour appealing for anyone from the area around the farm in Kent to contact the police. Every newspaper in the country carried a front-page statement from Bradshaw asking for people to come forward.

Within forty-eight hours the police had all the information Alan needed.

But when he went over the data, his worst fears were confirmed. . . .

The records showed that just under five miles from Dragon's Farm, there had been a Government Research Center, built after the War and used during the 1950s and early 1960s. The records did not reveal what the purpose of the building was, but Bradshaw, through General Harper, discovered this from the Ministry of Defense.

"Biological research," the inspector told Alan.

"In other words, biological warfare," Alan commented. "Killer chemicals and gases."

Bradshaw shrugged.

"Did they tell you what they were working on down there?"

The inspector shook his head. "I don't think they actually knew. We're trying to find the big shot who was in charge."

"Christ," Alan said in a flat, low voice. "God knows what they were doing down there. It could have been anything. They could have created that creature"—he nodded toward Charlie's cage—"by the use of radiation, chemicals—anything."

"What do you mean *created*? Sort of built it, you mean?" Bradshaw asked, disbelief evident in his question.

"Of course not. They could have been trying various

gases on spiders for some obscure reason, and produced by accident a mutant spider."

"But wouldn't they have killed it?"

"I don't know," Alan sighed. "There's only one way to find out."

"What's that?"

"Someone will have to go down there and look. . . ."

12

Alan himself volunteered to go down to Kent and investigate the disused Government building. But the trip was temporarily postponed. Bradshaw had found the man who used to be in charge of the research center, a Professor Colin Boyd. Boyd was living in the north of Scotland, where he had retired some years before. Bradshaw arranged for him to be brought to London.

Unbelievably, the professor had not even heard of the spider invasion. Having no radio or television, the elderly recluse did not even read the newspapers. He had only been traced after a nationwide hunt, and the discovery was due to the sharp wits of a local policeman who remembered the "strange auld fella" in the cottage in one of the remotest areas of Sutherland.

"He sounds nuts to me," Bradshaw said.

"Wouldn't you be? After the atrocities he's probably seen in his career, living in total isolation could be his only way of keeping any hold on sanity," Alan suggested. "Can you imagine? Spending one's life developing chemicals that maim, cripple, and destroy. Wouldn't you go a bit peculiar?"

"I suppose so," Bradshaw agreed. "Do you want to see any further statements from the people who lived near the farmhouse?"

Alan shook his head. "I've got enough. They all say the same thing, more or less. Though why no one took any action at the time is beyond me. Lambs, birds, calves, even the odd goat or two, all disappearing, or the occasional one found with the flesh stripped off its bones—that would make *me* worry."

"Farming folk are different," the inspector claimed. "As you've read, every one of them assumed it was a wild dog on the loose. All they wanted was to get the brute in the sights of their twelve-bores and then they reckoned the problem would be solved. You can't blame them. Even you wouldn't have believed *spiders* were responsible, would you?"

Alan had to agree.

Professor Boyd arrived the next day. He was a tall, gaunt man who had once been good-looking. There was a hidden strength in his crease-lined face. His trim white beard gave him the look of a sea captain rather than a leading biochemist.

But the scientis's eyes were troubled; they constantly darted from side to side, nervously. Alan had been correct in his assumption: the old man *had* seen too much. The pain in his eyes were a reflection of his memories.

Boyd sat in the small laboratory, his back to the caged spiders. When Alan had first shown him the creatures, the old man had almost fainted.

"It's all our fault," he kept murmuring, staring ahead as Alan led him to a chair. "We had no idea. No idea."

He refused to look at the spiders after that. He sat still, answering the questions Bradshaw and Alan flung at him, his body drooping, his hands hanging limply by his sides. A police secretary took shorthand notes of everything that was said.

"Suppose we start from the beginning, Professor Boyd," Bradshaw said.

"The beginning? What beginning?" the old man sighed. "The beginning is as old as man's need to kill—on as large a scale as possible. That's the beginning."

The inspector shifted uncomfortably in his chair. Raising his eyebrows, he glanced at Alan, who puck-

ered his brows and nodded slightly as if to say, "Let
him tell it in his own way."

"After the holocaust of the Second World War, the
Government gathered all the top scientists together at
some place near Hove. Physicists, chemists, bio-
chemists, nuclear scientists—they were all there," Boyd
went on.

"We were sworn to absolute secrecy and warned not
to repeat anything we were about to hear during the
three-day meeting. A talk was given by an Army
chap—I forget his name, but he was pretty high up—
about the Cold War and what it implied in terms of
military defense. To us scientists it didn't make much
sense; he went on about deploying defensive strategies
all over Europe against Russia. But we got the
message." The old man paused. Bradshaw and Alan
stared at him, riverted.

"The Russians were the Number One enemy. And if
we thought that the war had finished two years before,
we were all mistaken. This Army honcho pointed out
what was happening in Greece and Italy, and how the
Russians were behind it all. It would only be a matter
of time, he said, before they got around to Britain. And
then he raised our interest. He said that he had positive
proof that the Reds had not only a larger nuclear
stockpile, but had developed new sophisticated
methods of delivering atomic warheads.

"But then he told us that even the Russians were not
so stupid as to blow up one-half of the world just to
leave the other half filled with radiation. According to
the Army's sources—I suppose he meant spies—the
communists were years ahead of the West in the development of biological weapons."

"Do you mean chemical warfare techniques?" Alan
asked.

"Call it what you like," Boyd replied wearily. "The
use of toxins and gases to neutralize the enemy. Any-

way, we were told we had to develop our own systems along these lines. Money was no object. Oh yes, and the Americans would be working with us. Not physically, of course, but along their own lines, and there would be a cross-flow of information."

"Did no one object to this?" Alan queried.

"No one did," the professor said, shaking his head. "You must remember that we had all just lived through a war the likes of which mankind had never experienced. If we developed systems similar to the Russians, then, we believed, there would be less chance of another situation arising like that of 1939, when Britain and her allies were caught with hardly any defenses.

"With the carnage of Europe fresh in our minds, why should we object to anything that seemed likely to prevent another hell?"

Alan nodded. Given the situation, he wondered what he would have done.

"So the nuclear scientists went off to work on new types of atomic bombs, and the chemists and biologists were left to create a completely new type of weaponry. But it wasn't until 1952 that the Government built us a research center in Kent. They decided Kent was conveniently far enough away from London, so that if an accident happened there would be no public outcry; yet it was also near enough to the center to power and decision-making."

Alan saw Bradshaw frown with disgust. Professor Boyd could have been talking about the development of a new biscuit, the way he described the events.

"Yes, Professor," the inspector interrupted. "This is very interesting. But as we sit here there are thousands, if not millions, of spiders in the process of destroying the country. We'd like to know what exactly you did down at this research center."

"I'm coming to that," the old man said, lifting his

hands to his face. "I'm sorry. It's all been such a shock. . . ."

"Yes, of course," Bradshaw said without sympathy. "We've all had shocks. Will you go on, please."

"The idea was put forward by the military that a form of gas which killed human beings but kept the life-support systems intact could be an ultimate form of biological weapon. That meant the human population would be wiped out but livestock such as cows and sheep, and the whole insect and plant world necessary for ecological balance and the maintenance of life, would not be harmed. An army could then literally walk into a country and take it over with all the economic, industrial, agricultural and military advantages which related to it."

"Jesus," Alan muttered.

"Impossible," Bradshaw said.

"Impossible? Impossible you say?" Boyd asked, his eyes as bright as a madman's. "Oh, yes. That's what we thought! But let me tell you, my friends, that we came within a hair's breadth of achieving it. Yes, we almost succeeded. Almost succeeded . . ." his voice dropped and tailed off. Then the old man broke down, his body convulsed and racked with sobs.

Bradshaw looked at Alan, who sat stonyfaced, finding it impossible to feel sorry for Boyd. Alan had devoted his life to the study of biology, the science of living organisms, and this man beside him was coldly describing how he had almost succeeded in creating a destructive chemical that was more horrific in its concept and application than an atomic bomb.

No, he could not feel sympathy for Boyd. During the professor's description, Alan had been fighting the impulse to smash his fist into the old man's face. . . .

Neither man moved to aid the professor. It was their secretary, a young girl of about nineteen to whom the whole thing made no sense anyway, who poured some water into a cup and handed it to Boyd.

"I'm . . . I'm sorry," he mumbled eventually. "It's been so long. You see things differently from the distance of time."

Alan's expression did not alter.

"What exactly did you develop?" he asked flatly.

"We managed to synthesize a type of gas which was released through pressure pellets—that is, pellets which let the gas out at a controlled rate. They came later," he added almost apologetically, "from the military people. We used normal spray-guns. Anyway, it was found that the gas was not working properly. One of the constituents was setting up a chemical reaction. . . ."

"Hang on! Just a minute!" Alan peered at Boyd, cocking his head slightly. "Just what did you test this gas of yours on?"

The professor lowered his head to his chest, and shuffled his feet.

"I'd rather not answer that," he mumbled. "No. No, I won't answer that."

"The hell you will!" Bradshaw exploded, tired of Boyd's evasions, and started to stand up. Alan grabbed the inspector by the elbow and pulled him back.

"That's not going to achieve anything," Alan said quietly. "He's not an ordinary criminal, remember. He may not have known what he was doing."

"Oh, yes, young man," Boyd's voice sounded hollow, ghostly as he spoke, his chin sunk on his chest. "Oh, yes, we knew what we were doing. But we believed we were doing it for the eventual good of humanity."

Bradshaw sank back on his chair.

"Are you going to answer the question? What did you test this gas on?"

Boyd's chest heaved and he let out a long sigh.

"I suppose the truth had to come out sometime.

From what you tell me it's too late anyway. We . . .
we tested the gas on human beings, of course."

"Jesus Christ!" Bradshaw hissed.

Alan felt all strength drain out of him.

Even the secretary looked up in disbelief, her pencil
poised over the notebook.

"We tested the gas on human beings," Boyd repeated, as if to make sure they had heard correctly.
"Madmen beyond any hope; terminal cancer patients
with only days or weeks to live; war-wounded soldiers
who were vegetables. We were very selective."

Alan felt the strength return to him. The strength of
hatred. He grasped the sides of his chair, his knuckles
turning white, and then slowly began to rise. There was
only one thought in his mind—to kill the old man in
front of him.

Bradshaw grasped his arm tight, and murmured,
"Don't! I know how you feel, but we still need to know
what happened. Over fifty million lives depend on what
he's going to tell us."

The reasoning filtered through to Alan's mind and
he sat down.

"Just one more thing," he said, his teeth clenched.
"How many . . . did you murder?"

"About twenty or thirty," Boyd answered. "I can't
remember. There were three of us involved and two
Army guys. The other two scientists are dead now. I
don't know about the Army people," he added and
suddenly looked up, eyes ablaze. "But hear this before
you condemn me!" he said forcefully. "These men and
women—yes, women—were practically dead or living
a death much worse than you can imagine in your wild-
est nightmares. I saw soldiers without arms or legs,
their faces burned beyond recognition, sigh with relief
when they realized they were about to die! I've seen
maniacs, frothing at the mouth, become calm and smile
as they, too, saw their escape through death! Don't

condemn me, when your generation has condoned the use of napalm against innocent villagers in Vietnam!" Boyd slumped back in his chair, his energy almost spent.

"I didn't condone it," Alan muttered, all anger now gone as he realized that the old man's words contained certain seeds of truth.

"Can we get back to the spiders, please?" said Bradshaw coldly. "What did you find out about this gas of yours?"

"It worked on humans all right. They died within minutes. Cattle were unaffected, as planned. The basic life-support system—the insects like flies, mites, midges, ants, ladybirds, and so on—were wiped out. But *not* spiders," he emphasized slowly.

"*Not* the spiders," Alan pondered. "Only the food they relied on—the other small insects."

"Exactly," Boyd nodded. "We were at a complete loss to explain this, apart from the reason I gave before, about one of the chemicals reacting in a random fashion."

"Where did you test the gas?" Bradshaw's practical police-trained mind was at work.

"Oh, we had a section of the grounds wired off," Boyd answered simply, with a wave of his hand.

"What did you do after discovering the gas was useless?" Alan asked.

"Not useless, please. Merely malfunctioning at a certain level," the professor insisted. "We collected as many spiders as we could in an attempt to find out why they were immune. We had a biologist on the team, and he arranged for some spiders to be sent from abroad which, he claimed, we could test more easily. . . ."

"Spiders from Pakistan, for example, like Stegodyphus?"

"Yes, I think that was one species. We had all sorts.

It's not my field of study, so I can't be sure how many types there were. But we noticed one strange thing," Boyd added. "The second generation of British spiders—the offspring of parents which had been exposed to the gas—had harder bodies and seemed slightly larger."

"When was all this?" Bradshaw asked.

"In the mid-sixties. Just before we closed down."

"Thanks. It's for the records," he explained automatically. "Go on."

"It looked as if the gas had affected the hormones in the parent spiders, producing a mutation which would naturally be passed on to the spiderlings."

"That figures," Alan nodded, leaning over to Bradshaw. "Spiders' growth and moulting *are* completely controlled by hormones," he explained.

"Even though we tried all sorts of experiments there was no explanation as to why the spiders were immune. Someone suggested that it had something to do with their poison glands. . . . I don't know," the old man shook his head.

"We don't have enough knowledge about a spider's chemical makeup as yet," Alan muttered, as if to himself. "It could be something to do with the venom, but who knows? I don't think it matters now. Did anything else happen down at this hellhole of yours?" he asked Boyd.

"Yes. One other thing. In the middle of this research there was a fire. The military thought it was sabotage, but I suppose the truth will never be known. Practically everything was destroyed: files, equipment and, so we believed, all the spiders we had been experimenting with. Obviously they weren't. After that the research center closed down, and we were sent to other parts of the country.

"And that, gentlemen, is all I can tell you." Professor Boyd ended, looking from one to the other.

The room was still for a few minutes. Alan was trying to grasp the horror of what the professor had said. Bradshaw, quite simply, was incredulous. The secretary had sharpened her pencil.

"Thank you, Professor Boyd," Bradshaw said finally. "I don't know if it helps, but at least it gives us something to go on. Now if you'll excuse us. . . ."

"Of course, of course," Boyd interrupted. "I'd like to sit here for a few minutes. I feel rather weak."

Bradshaw nodded and indicated to Alan to follow him out of the room. The two men and the secretary paused in the corridor.

"Have that typed up quickly, please," Bradshaw instructed the girl. "Where can we talk without being disturbed?" he asked, turning to Alan.

"In here," Alan pointed to a door on the left. "It's my private office."

They entered a small book-filled room. Papers were strewn over the desk and a number of bottles, containing small spiders in formaldehyde solution, stood lined on a shelf.

"What do you make of it, Alan? Is the old guy round the bend? Or do you think all that really happened?"

"I think he's mad, but no more insane than the politicians and military men who thought the whole thing up. After what he did, can you now understand why he'd want to cut himself off from the rest of the world?"

"Right. But what about the spiders? What happened to make them the way they are?"

"The professor was fairly near the mark when he said they didn't all die in the fire," Alan said, doodling absentmindedly on a pad in front of him. "The way I see it—and I'm thinking out loud here—the majority of them actually escaped. So you've got a bunch of different species of spider running around in an area that's had all the insect life destroyed all except spiders. The new mutant spiders would therefore have to eat other spiders; and for some reason, and this is by no means impossible, the Pakistani, British, and God knows what other kinds of spiders would start crossbreeding."

Alan paused, picturing in his mind the situation, so many years before, as new mutant spiders, their sex glands and hormones affected by the gas, began to breed.

"It takes a few years for a completely new species to appear. With their natural environment totally screwed up, the spiders would have to adapt themselves, change their structure in various ways."

"What about food?" the inspector asked, fascinated and at the same time horrified by the picture Alan was drawing.

"Mice, moles, birds, rats—anything they could get their poison fangs into," Alan said. "Which I reckon would account for the development of their sharp, flesh-tearing teeth."

He picked up one of the specimen jars and peered closely at the spider inside.

"Yes, I reckon that's what happened," he sighed. "And as the wildlife in the immediate vicinity became scarce, they would go further afield, looking for more food. Dogs, cats, chickens, calfs, lambs—everything that we've heard your witnesses mention disappearing."

"Where to now?" Bradshaw asked.

"I'd like to see the people who lived in Dragon's Farm before my parents bought it. They disappeared suddenly, it seems, about a year ago. Why?" Alan looked at Bradshaw. "Can you organize that?"

The inspector nodded.

"Anything else?" he queried.

"I still want to go down to that ex-Government building. To see if . . ."

He was interrupted by a scream from the laboratory—a broken, gasping howl. They rushed through the door, Bradshaw instinctively pulling out a revolver.

In the corner beside one of the cages lay Professor Boyd. And on his body, sinking its biting jaws into his throat, stood a large, pulsating spider.

Alan and Bradshaw watched as the spider pulled away flesh, exposing the professor's larynx and ending the old man's cries with shocking suddenness.

Bradshaw dropped to one knee and, holding the gun in front of him with two hands, took steady aim. The gunshot reverberated around the lab and the spider was flung a few feet up in the air and against a wall, where it slid to the floor, a bloody, hairy pile. Its legs quivered for a few seconds and then were still.

Alan knelt by Professor Boyd, but it was too late. Life flowed out of the elderly man as quickly and smoothly as the blood from his throat. Tears flowed down Boyd's cheeks as he looked at Alan. The old man shook his head, grabbed Alan's wrist tightly, tried to pull himself up, but collapsed back on the floor, his head rolling loosely to the side. He was dead.

Alan freed himself from the vicelike grip and stood up. He went across to the cage.

"Look," he said hoarsely.

Bradshaw saw that the top of the glass cage had been smashed with a stone paperweight.

"He did it deliberately," Alan almost whispered. "He committed suicide. He wanted to die," he added, shaking his head.

"After what he told us, do you blame him?"

Alan did not reply. He was wondering how many other people had been driven to death in the name of science and progress. . . .

13

After Bradshaw had left to organize the search for the previous owners of the farmhouse, Alan slowly made his way up to the living quarters at the top of the building. Previously executive suites, they had been converted into ten separate bedrooms which, with the washrooms on the same floor, provided comfortable temporary accommodation for the scientists and civil servants of the Action Team. There was a communal dining room on the floor below, formerly a directors' lunchroom.

Alan glanced into the dining room to check if Louise was there. Not seeing her, he continued upstairs to their bedroom.

She was sitting on the bed, her hands clasped tightly, a worried look on her face.

"What's wrong, love?" Alan asked.

"Mom," she said simply.

"What's happened to her?" Alan could not hide the concern in his voice. He had only met Louise's mother a few times, at her home up in Sale, near Manchester, but had got along very well with the elderly lady.

"Nothing's happened," Louise said, shaking her head. "It's just that she's now too terrified even to leave the house. And she's worried sick about me. God, I wish Dad was still alive."

"Why won't she leave the house?" he asked, already knowing the answer, as he sat down and put his arm around Louise.

"The spiders, of course. She says she sees them all over the place. Can't sleep at night. And when she does doze off during the day, she says she dreams of hundreds of spiders crawling over her body in the dark." Louise frowned. "She's got it bad, Alan. Really bad."

"What can we do?"

"I don't know. But I feel I should go up and visit her. At least that way she'll see *I'm* OK."

Alan looked troubled.

"Well, I suppose, if you must. . . . But I do need you here. Not just for me, but because of the work. We're on to something new." He outlined the professor's story and described what had happened in the lab.

"I did suggest to Mom that she fly to Montreal. Her sister's over there. And when this trouble's over—if ever—she could come back," Louise explained, leaning heavily against Alan. He smelled a light whiff of perfume, but fought the rising surge of desire he felt.

"Good idea. What did she say to that?"

"There's no way she can get a ticket. People are camping at Manchester airport in the hope of getting abroad. And the airport authorities said on the radio this morning that it would take at least a year to clear the list of the people wanting tickets now."

"That's no problem," Alan said confidently. "I'll get Sir Stanley on to it. We'll fix up a ticket for her. He owes us something."

Louise's face brightened. "You think you can?"

"Of course," he replied. "And you've got to go up there and see her. Take her to the airport. My car's downstairs. You'd better drive up—but don't open the windows. Keep them tightly shut all the way. I don't trust those hairy bastards; the next thing we know they'll be flying."

Louise kissed him tenderly and began preparing for her journey. Alan watched her drive off, blowing kisses at him. As most of the gas stations had been left unattended, she filled the car herself at one self-service garage and set off for the M1. At first the roads were deserted, but as she neared the outer edges of London, she noticed mobs of people roaming the streets, smashing shop windows and ransacking houses.

Taking the North Circular Road around London, she stopped automatically at a set of traffic lights, waiting for them to turn green. About half a dozen teenagers, wearing black leather jackets and carrying wine bottles, appeared suddenly from a house to her left and surrounded the car. Two of them stood in front while the others began rocking the car from side to side.

She began to scream, which made the young thugs laugh louder. Shouting obscenities, they tried to open the doors of her car. Luckily Louise had locked them all when she was closing the windows.

The car rocked dangerously, and Louise realized it would soon turn over. She glanced at the two drunken youths leering over the hood. There was no choice. Slamming the gear into first, she gunned the engine and shot forward, the rear tires squealing.

One of the teenagers spun off to the side, but the other, sprawled across the front of the car, grabbed a wing-mirror with one hand and tried to smash the windshield with his wine bottle. Louise slammed on the brakes, then almost immediately put her foot down hard on the accelerator.

The sudden jolt knocked the boy forward and on to the ground. Before he could stand, the car had run over him. Louise felt the crunch of tires against the youth's ribs and, glancing in her rear mirror, saw him lying in the road, grasping his stomach, a red puddle rapidly forming around him.

Sobbing, she drove like a maniac the rest of the way to the M1, not stopping for lights or at intersections. Once on the motorway she slowed down, pulled into the hard shoulder, stumbled out of the car, and was sick.

Twenty miles out of London the traffic began to build up, and soon Louise was crawling along at 30 mph. At each service stop, police waved the traffic on, only allowing those who needed gas into the stopovers. Fortunately her car had a Top Priority pass on the windshield, as issued to all members of Action Team. Realizing it could take her over ten hours to reach Manchester, she pulled in beside a police car.

She produced her own identification and indicated the pass on the windshield.

"I don't know what we can do, miss," he said grimly. "It's sheer hell on those roads. But I'll talk to the chief about it."

She waited ten minutes until the policeman returned with an older man with silver epaulets on his dark uniform.

"Afternoon, miss," the old man said. "I'm Superintendent Brown. I've just been in touch with London, and they've cleared you. I spoke to Inspector Bradshaw and we'll try and get you up to Manchester as quickly as we can."

Louise smiled with relief.

"Thank you," she said, "but how?" waving her arm at the solid line of traffic filling all four lanes.

"We'll use the emergency lane. Sergeant Wilkins will lead the way in his car, and you can follow. Good luck."

The drive was exhausting. Cars had broken down and pulled into the hard shoulder. This meant the policemen in front of Louise had to get out and stop the traffic on the inside lane—a dangerous and tricky business, as drivers and passengers alike saw every delay as making them more likely to be overtaken by the spiders.

Eventually she reached Sale. Her mother, visibly trembling as she cautiously opened the door, burst into tears when she saw Louise.

The house looked smaller than Louise remembered it, and there was a musty smell. She went to open a window.

"Don't!" her mother screamed. "The spiders! They'll get in."

Louise left the window closed and helped her mother pack. Alan had phoned earlier and informed Mrs. Roberts that he had arranged an air ticket for her.

They left for the airport almost immediately. The plane was due to take off in ninety minutes and Louise had no idea what traffic problems they would run into. But it was not traffic that held them up. It was people.

Huge crowds were gathered around the airport. They had to leave their car with hundreds of other abandoned vehicles, and they walked the final half-mile to the terminal. Slowly they made their way between tents, caravans, and open fires. It was a camp of despair. No laughter enlivened the night air, no sounds of music.

Everyone knew it was only a matter of time before the spiders reached the Midlands. Some estimates gave Manchester a month before invasion. Others said sooner. But for the people camped around the airport it could as likely be tomorrow, judging from the desperation on their faces.

At last Louise and her mother reached the terminal and picked their way through the huddled groups lying asleep on every floor.

"I'm collecting a ticket for Mrs. Daphne Roberts, flying to Montreal," she informed the girl behind the British Airways counter.

"Hang on and I'll check," the girl replied, her voice tired and flat. She picked up a sheet in front of her.

"Is this a Special Priority from London?" she asked.

"Yes, from Sir Stanley Jenson," Louise nodded.

"Sign here, please," the girl said, pushing a form unenthusiastically across the desk.

Mrs. Roberts sighed the foot of the page, her hand still shaking.

The girl leaned across the counter. "The flight's due to leave in half an hour," she whispered. "There won't be an announcement. When this all first started," she raised her eyebrows at the crowds, "we announced one transatlantic flight and crowds rushed the plane. We had to call the police in before it could take off. That's why there are police at every door now."

Louise glanced at the departure lounge. Scores of policemen stood around the room, each with a gun strapped to an open holster.

"Thank you," she said quietly. "We'll be ready to board on time."

"Have you got your passport?" the girl wanted to know.

Mrs. Roberts nodded and went to fish it out of her handbag.

"I don't want it. But you'll need it for identification before you can get on the plane. We've had a few murders, with people being battered to death for their tickets."

Louise felt sick as she guided her mother to the departure lounge. They hugged one another and she watched her mother disappear through the lines of policemen and out to the waiting plane.

With difficulty Louise found her way back to the car. Driving to an open spot about a mile away from the airport, she stopped and looked back, waiting to see the plane take off which carried her mother to safety.

Apart from spiders, Mrs. Robert's greatest phobia was flying. She had traveled in an airplane only once before in her life, when she went with her late husband on a holiday to Spain. But then, she reminded herself as she sat in the huge Jumbo jet, Douglas had been there to hold her hand and assure her that everything was all right.

Now she was alone, surrounded by strangers. She wished the journey were over and that she were sitting having tea with her sister, whom she had not seen for eight years.

Mrs. Roberts twisted the straps of her handbag nervously. She thought of Louise and prayed she would be safe from the spiders. The thought of them still made her shudder convulsively.

The jet engines roared noisily, and she shuddered again. They were moving. She checked her seatbelt for the tenth time and clung tightly to the narrow armrests.

"Thank God we're getting out of that mess, eh?" said a large, well-dressed man beside her.

Mrs. Roberts nodded dumbly.

"Nervous?"

She nodded again.

"Don't worry. These are great planes. Flew them often in the old days."

The old days! The implications of the phrase did not escape Mrs. Roberts.

"Anyway," the man went on, "it's better than being eaten alive by spiders." He laughed.

Mrs. Roberts managed a brave smile.

"Yes, you're right, I suppose," she said, trying not to think of Louise returning to London.

As the plane lifted off Mrs. Roberts gulped in fear. But the whine of the engines soon died to a low hum as they leveled off.

"Good evening, ladies and gentlemen," a voice crackled over the intercom. "This is Captain MacGregor speaking. On behalf of the crew, I welcome you aboard and hope you have an enjoyable flight to Montreal. We will be stopping in about half an hour for

fuel. You're probably aware of the rules forbidding refueling at Manchester. I'll report on our position from
time to time. Enjoy your flight."

The jovial man next to Mrs. Roberts nodded.

"Probably landing in France or Holland," he said.
"Damn nuisance this refueling regulation."

Mrs. Roberts agreed, not really caring where they
refueled as long as she could get to her sister.

Refueling at Manchester had ceased for two reasons.
Before the new rules, the planes had stood on the tarmac for a few hours at least, and this was too much of
a temptation for the waiting crowds. At the start they
had mobbed the planes, the police being no match for
the crazed refugees desperate to board the plane.

Secondly, some people had ambushed the service
and fuel vehicles, changing into the uniforms of the
mechanics they overpowered. Then they had driven
through the checkpoints out to the planes and boarded
them, refusing to budge. Some of them had carried
guns, so again there was nothing the police could do.

For security, it was decided to stop all refueling at
Manchester—and to give the police weapons. The
crowds quieted down after that.

For added security, pilots would not divulge to the
passengers where they intended refueling. In this case
it was not France or Holland, as most people expected,
but deserted Heathrow, which had closed down after
the reappearance of the spiders. After thorough aerial
reconnaissance had been carried out, the authorities
were satisfied that the area was now clear of spiders.
As the insects marched northward, there seemed no
reason for them to linger in what was now a virtual
wasteland, devoid of living prey. The fact that Heathrow
was now being used as a massive fuel station was kept
from the public to avoid potential panic among flying
passengers. Troops guarded the airport, and planes

came and went frequently. Servicing, however, was carried out abroad.

Mrs. Roberts settled back in her seat and tried to sleep, hoping that when she awoke they would be in Canada.

Down below Louise had watched the lights of the plane twinkle into the distance. She smiled, and started the long drive back to London along the almost deserted southbound motorway. . . .

Mrs. Roberts woke with a jolt as the plane's wheels hit the runway at Heathrow. For a moment she wondered where she was and then remembered the pilot's words about fuel.

"Are we in France?" she asked the big man next to her.

He shrugged.

"Can't say. It's too dark to see," he said. "Here comes the tanker," he added, pointing out the window. "It's a British Airways truck anyway, so we're in good hands," he laughed.

The fueling operation had been worked out to the last detail. Pilots contacted Heathrow to announce their arrival. As they landed, fuel tankers began speeding across the runways, often moving alongside the planes before they had stopped. Each tanker's windows had been replaced with aluminum sheets and the doors could be opened only from the inside. A mechanic, dressed in a fire-fighting outfit, jumped out of the truck and connected a hose to the plane, returning to the tanker as soon as he had checked the connections and flow. Once the plane was fully loaded, he disconnected and drove away. No one was taking any chances.

On the night of Mrs. Robert's flight, dark rain clouds filled the sky. The two mechanics sat in the cab of the tanker, staring ahead, their vision restricted by their visors and the sealed windows.

They watched the needle on the fuel gauge rise

steadily and then stop automatically as the plane reached its optimum load. One of them jumped out and unhooked the long, thick hose. It began to rain as he hurried back to the tanker with its headlights shining into the dark. He glanced back at the plane and waved, but the streaming rain on his visor made clear vision impossible.

Even if it had not been raining, it is doubtful whether he would have seen the black rivulets adhering to the undercarriage, and streaming in through the flaps of the wheels and the elevator flaps under the tail.

It was a dark night. . . .

The plane lifted off smoothly and the pilot guided it slowly westward, swinging around in an arc. They had traveled only about fifty miles when one of the jets stuttered and decreased in power.

"Shit!" the captain swore. "Looks like we've got bloody birds in the engine," he said and increased the power of the jet thrust. After a few seconds the engine ran normally, so he sat back in relief.

Then he pressed the stewardess button to order some coffee. Nothing happened. He pressed it again, wondering what had happened to the girl. He looked at his copilot, shrugged, and made a few minor adjustments. She would come eventually, he told himself.

Mrs. Roberts was sitting in one of the aisle seats near the back of the plane, gazing blankly ahead. She was thinking about the strange twists and turns that her life had taken. Mrs. Roberts had never asked a lot from life. She had grown up in a family that owned a small newspaper and candy store and she had never gone hungry, but she had never known luxury either. When her parents died, she had inherited a small sum of money which she and her husband used as a deposit for their first home.

Mr. Roberts had died a few years previously, from a heart attack. Though at first lonely, she gradually began to build up a new life for herself, joining pensioners' clubs and taking part in church activities. She was proud of Louise, her only child, and looked forward to the day when her daughter was married and Mrs. Roberts could spend her old age surrounded by grandchildren. At sixty-three Mrs. Roberts had reached the age when ambition was just a word, but hopes were a reality.

She opened the large handbag on her lap and pulled out a ball of wool and knitting needles. She still felt very nervous at being in a plane. Knitting would calm her down. And an extra sweater would come in handy for the cold winters in Canada.

She peered closely at the pattern she had taken from the bag. Her eyes were not as good as they used to be, and she screwed them up, focusing on the small print. Apart from her gray hair, this was the only real sign of impending old age. Her small, cheery face had only a few wrinkles. A fastidiously neat and smart dresser, she looked all of ten years younger than she was.

The stewardess, a pleasant young Canadian with blonde hair and sparkling white teeth, stopped by Mrs. Robert's seat.

"Is everything all right?" she asked.

"Oh, yes, thank you. It's not as bad as I thought it would be," Mrs. Roberts replied with a small grimace.

"Do you want to keep your seatbelt on during the journey?" the girl smiled.

"Oh, heavens, yes. Of course."

"Well, if you'll let me tighten it a little, I think you'll feel safer," the stewardess said, leaning over and adjusting the loose straps. "There. Is that too tight?"

"No, thank you. It's perfect," Mrs. Roberts nodded.

"Good luck with your knitting," the girl said, walking down the aisle toward the front of the plane, checking passengers as she did so.

Mrs. Roberts went to put her bag on the floor

beneath her feet. As she did, the ball of wool toppled off her knees and rolled slowly to the back of the plane, unwinding as it did.

"Blast it," she muttered, and twisted around, watching the wool move away from her. It stopped outside the toilet door.

Mrs. Roberts was about to call the stewardess for help when she thought she saw something spilling under the door. Something resembling black, seeping oil. It spread quickly, pouring toward her seat.

She screwed her eyes up tightly, and with shocking clarity the black pool took shape. Spiders!

She gasped aloud, then half croaked, half screamed as the insects came within a few feet of her seat. She tried to stand up, but could not. She was trapped, bound in by her seatbelt.

"Spiders! Spiders!" she screamed.

For a few seconds there was a stunned silence, then the first wave of panic broke. The man beside Mrs. Roberts jumped up and pushed past her, treading on her feet as he went by. He rushed down the aisle. A stewardess—the one who had spoken to Mrs. Roberts—showed amazing presence of mind by grabbing a fire extinguisher and directing it at the oncoming spiders. A powerful spray of white foam halted the creatures' advance for a moment. But it was too late for Mrs. Roberts. The spreading army had already reached her.

She felt the spiders move across her ankles and up her legs. When the first one crawled over her knee and along the inside of her thigh, she closed her legs, feeling the creature trapped between her soft flesh wriggle and bite. She screamed until she was breathless, and then exhausted, slumping back in her seat, her head lolling to one side, saliva dribbling from the corner of her mouth, her eyes bulging and staring ahead in a fixed trance of shock.

Through the rest of the plane, the spiders poured among the hysterical passengers, some of whom were trying to open the emergency hatch. A stewardess who tried to reach the hatch was hit in the face and knocked to the ground, where the insects greedily clambered over her.

Men and women pulled, fought, and scratched each other. They knew it was hopeless. There was nowhere to go. One man tried to put his fist through the dou-be-glazed window, but only broke his wrist.

Gradually everyone retreated into the first-class section. Another stewardess, having seen the effect of the fire extinguisher, moved forward with another. She sprayed the spiders vigorously, but they seemed to ignore the foam and still advanced on her, climbing up her legs and over her body.

She ran back screaming, the spiders clinging, through the berserk passengers and into the pilot's cabin. The captain, copilot, and flight engineer looked up startled from their control panels.

They heard the stewardess screaming something, but could not make out what she was saying. They did not have to. The spiders on her uniform told them all they needed to know.

The hysterical girl was propelled forward as dazed passengers tried to crowd into the cockpit, looking for safety. Captain MacGregor tried to push them back, but someone rammed an elbow into his stomach and winded him, knocking him over his seat. Glancing downward he could see a black tide enter the cockpit and fan out.

One passenger was pushing every button in sight as spiders crawled over his head. The plane began to go into a spin, and keeled forward, throwing all those in the cockpit on top of each other.

"Let me get to the controls!" MacGregor yelled.

"We'll be over Bristol in a few minutes. We've got to get out to sea!"

No one took any notice of him. The copilot was slumped over his console, blood pouring from his neck. The flight engineer was lost under a pile of struggling bodies. MacGregor pulled and clawed his way to the radio, and pressed a button on the panel.

"Mayday. Mayday. Flight BA 421. Mayday. Spiders taken over. Spiders taken over. Am trying to . . ." his voice trailed off as he saw the lights of central Bristol rush dizzily up toward him. . . .

As its wings grazed a church tower, the jet burst into flames in midair. Just before it hit the ground it exploded—causing widespread death and destruction across the city.

There were no survivors. Not even a spider.

14

"You can't blame yourself," Alan said softly to Louise. "You didn't know. How could you have known? Keeping Heathrow open! Even *we* weren't told." He shook his head angrily.

"And all those innocent people in Bristol," she cried, her eyes red. "It's so awful. If only I'd told Mom to stay where she was."

At least 110 people had died in Bristol—plus the full load of 450 passengers, and ten crew in the jumbo jet.

Louise looked up at Alan from their bed, where she had huddled miserably since hearing the news of her mother's death.

"Whatever you're doing to try and stop these filthy creatures, I want to be part of it," she said.

"You are, my love, you are," he said, soothingly stroking her hair. "I told you that before you went to Manchester."

She shook her head.

"No, I don't mean just taking notes, preparing solutions, or making coffee. Something more positive, more active," she insisted.

"I don't know what you can do," Alan said. "I don't know what anyone can do," he added.

Louise was not put off.

"I want to be with you all the way," she said, her eyes narrowing. "Go where you go, do what you do. These monsters killed my mother!"

"And my dad," Alan said quietly, he lowered his head and rested his cheeks against Louise's warm, tear-dampened face.

Just before news of the crash came through, Bradshaw had phoned Alan to tell him that the previous owners of Dragon's Farm had been traced.

"But there's a snag," he added. "They refuse to come to London. They say they're not leaving their new farm and if we want to talk to them we've got to go to Wales and see them."

"Wales?" Alan echoed. "It'll take us nearly a day to get there!"

"Well, that's it. They're absolutely firm and won't be moved. *And* they don't have a phone. I got the message through the local policeman. So it's up to you, Alan," the inspector said. "I can lay a car on if you think it's important."

Alan reflected for a few seconds. Apart from Boyd, there had been no real breakthrough. Anything was worth a chance at this stage.

"We'll go," he said. "Tomorrow."

The crash had interfered with that plan. But when Alan told Louise he was going to Wales the following day, she insisted on joining him. He agreed, thinking the drive might be good for her.

In a remote corner of north Wales the Kendricks, former owners of Dragon's Farm, had taken over a rundown place and were trying to bring it up to standard.

The Kendricks were a proud, independent family. Frank Kendrick, now head of the family, was a tall, strong, broad man with large hands. Farming hands. Not for him the niceties of "gentleman farming," where a landowner hired labor and never so much as got soil on his hands or dirt under his fingernails, he later told them when Louise politely asked him what sort of farm he had. No, Frank Kendrick was a man who worked long and hard, and never questioned why. His family had been farmers for generations. It was their way.

His wife, Margaret, felt the same. She too, was descended from farming folk of the rough, tough, and hard-working type. She was small, rounded, and had given Frank four children—three sons and a daughter.

Both sets of their parents lived with them in the rambling Welsh farmhouse. This also was their way.

But Frank Kendrick was not at home when Alan first arrived with Bradshaw and Louise.

"He's doing the fence in the south field," Margaret Kendrick told them. "You're quite welcome to wait. But I can't sit and talk to you. I've got to make the supper."

They looked at each other, smiling. Bradshaw, who was used to country manners, thought nothing of it. But Louise, feeling very touchy anyway, complained quietly that they had not even been offered a cup of tea.

"It all depends whether Frank likes us or not," Bradshaw explained. "He's the head of the house, the provider. If he says we can have a cup of tea, then we'll have a cup of tea."

Alan and Louise wandered outside.

"Beautiful, isn't it?" he murmured, putting an arm around her and drawing her close to him.

"Mmm," she nodded.

The green hills swept down to a deep valley crisscrossed with rivers and streams. A thick wood spread across ten miles; above it tall, pointed, powerful mountains loomed into the sky. It was certainly one of the pleasantest scenes either of them had seen in months.

For Alan it brought home how much there was to lose if the spiders won their insane battle against man.

"How would you like to live out here?" Alan asked gently, feeling Louise's warm body against his side. He hugged her closer.

"It would be heaven—with you," she whispered, her eyes wide as she looked up at him.

For the first time in weeks, all the knots of tension

left Alan's body and he pulled Louise around to face him. There was no desperation, no naked lust in his kiss as he held her pressed against him.

The two had grown even closer over the previous few weeks. The death of Louise's mother had affected Alan in a strange way. Somehow he felt responsible for Louise, telling himself that he had to look after her. Louise was aware of these feelings and, far from rejecting them, welcomed Alan's concern.

They returned to the car and sat with Bradshaw, discussing this and that. Frank Kendrick appeared two hours later, his boots spattered with mud, carrying a large mallet.

He completely ignored the car and walked past it into the house. They followed him in.

"Mr. Kendrick?" Bradshaw queried.

"Yes, that's me," the tall farmer said. "What do you want?"

"We want to talk to you about Dragon's Farm," the inspector told him.

Kendrick squinted at Alan and Louise before answering.

"I don't want to talk about it," he said, turning away. "You've wasted your time coming up here. Good-bye."

"Mr. Kendrick, we've come a long way," Bradshaw explained. "From London in fact."

"Well, that's your concern. Not mine," Kendrick gruffly said. "I just don't want to talk about the farm."

"Why not?" Alan questioned.

"Because I've had enough of it! Because . . ."

"Because of the spiders?" prompted Alan.

Kendrick breathed in sharply, and then nodded slowly.

"Yes, and the other things."

"The other things!" Bradshaw and Alan echoed simultaneously.

"Aye, the other things," he repeated. "But I'm not going to talk. It's finished. Over."

"Mr. Kendrick," Louise said quietly. "It's not finished. It won't be finished for a long time yet. And when it is over there won't be *anything* left. No animals, no men, no women and . . ." she glanced out of the window at the Kendrick children ". . . no children."

Frank Kendrick stared fiercely at Louise for a few seconds before gesturing to some chairs.

"Sit down, will you," he said. "I'll tell you what I know."

Alan sighed with relief.

"Did you notice anything unusual in the last few years?" he asked when they were seated.

"Oh, yes," Kendrick nodded slowly. "We saw it all. We saw the spiders. We saw them kill our livestock."

"You saw them! And you didn't report it! I don't believe it!" Alan said in an angry tone. "Do you know what's happened?"

Frank Kendrick looked directly at Alan. The farmer's eyes were hooded and blank.

"I know. But let me have my say first."

He glanced at his wife.

"Margaret, you don't want to be hearing this again. Why don't you go in the kitchen and make us some tea."

Margaret Kendrick shuffled out of the room.

"What exactly did you see?" Bradshaw asked.

"As I said—the spiders. Hundreds of them one morning crawling over one of my newly born calves. Its mother was like a mad dog, and I came into the field just as the spiders started to climb over her. I was rabbiting at the time and shot the poor beast with a spray of lead. The spiders scattered after that. I thought they'd gone, but one morning I found what was left of Rusty, our dog, and knew they were back."

"How long ago was this?" Bradshaw wanted to know.

"Just over a year ago. Before we moved out."

"Why *did* you move out and why the hell didn't you tell the police about the spiders?" Alan demanded.

Kendrick smiled wistfully, and chuckled.

"You city folk don't understand, do you?" he said. "My father, and grandfather, and his father, and *his* father before him farmed that land with no trouble or interference. Then these folk from the city with their fancy machines arrived and put up fences where there had been fields, concrete where there had been grass and flowers, and brought poison gases and killer sprays in place of the fresh air." He paused, his face stony.

No one stirred, moved up the man's vivid description.

"And because of all that, everything was upset. The land was not the same, the earth was being killed. And you see, we're on the side of Nature. The soil is in our blood. We felt what was happening without knowing all the big words you city folk call it. We knew that you can't muck about with Nature and expect nothing to happen. It's Nature's way, sir," he concluded, looking at Alan. "And no one will change *that* fact."

It was an emotional, if unscientific argument for ecology, the natural balance of all life on earth. Alan saw the flaws, but he could not tell the farmer. Because, deep down, Alan agreed with Kendrick. You could not muck about with Nature and expect things to remain the same.

"What finally made you leave?" he asked.

Kendrick looked around at the kitchen door before replying.

"I don't want Margaret to hear this again. It's bad enough trying to live with it now," he commented. "She had another baby two years ago—another girl. One day it was in its carriage in the garden. I don't know what happened exactly—I was in one of the fields—but I heard Margaret's screams from over a mile away. The spiders got the baby," he said flatly. "And Margaret saw it. They picked the wee child clean. I buried it, so I know. After that, we'd had enough. This was Nature's way of telling us. And we were angry. We wanted others to suffer as we had. We had lost nearly everything—our livestock was being killed, and we were not going to risk our other children's lives. So now you know. Do you blame us? Or do you still not understand?"

Alan gripped the edge of the chair, understanding only too well. He noticed Louise had gone white, tears forming in her eyes. He knew how she would react if she had seen her baby eaten by the spiders. She would have wanted revenge. Just like the Kendricks.

Only Bradshaw seemed unaffected, and he relentlessly pursued his questioning.

"These 'other things' you mentioned. What were they?"

Kendrick sighed.

"A while after I'd seen the calf killed, I was going through the fields one morning. I wanted to move our bull from one field to another, for it was nearly time for him to mate. I found the bull all right. He was lying on the ground, covered with spiders. But the beast wasn't dead and the spiders weren't picking at his flesh. They were different, these spiders, not black but a sort of light brown.

"I let off a shot from my rifle, into the air, and they scattered. I went over to my bull. He lay panting on the ground, but apart from a few bites on his side he seemed all right. . . ."

"What size were these spiders?" Alan wanted to know.

"Oh, they were big. About the size of a man's fist. Anyway, the bull got up and walked off. I took him to a new field, and the next morning I looked in on him. There was nothing wrong with him as far as I could see, so I thought it would be safe to put him with the cows. That afternoon I went down to the field to bring the cows back for milking. Three were dead, their stomachs ripped open, and a fourth lay bellowing while the bull tore bits of hide and guts from her. I went and got my gun and shot the beast dead.

"We left Dragon's Farm after that," he ended.

Only the quiet tick of a clock could be heard after Frank Kendrick had finished his tale. His wife came in with a tray laden with mugs of tea and piled high with cakes, but no one felt like eating.

They left soon afterward and drove back to London, silent for most of the journey. . . .

15

The Action Committee shuffled papers nervously. Only half of the original forty members remained; the others had resigned under pressure from their families, or just stopped turning up. They sat in the conference room of the ex-chemical company building which housed the Action Team.

A special meeting had been called on Alan's insistence to report on the latest findings. Rumor had spread that more bad news was on the way. With the spiders massing along the Thames valley and around through Buckinghamshire and Hertfordshire, London was surrounded and the creatures were rapidly closing in on the center from all sides.

Most of the population had gone, leaving London quiet except for the army tanks and trucks which rumbled through the streets in search of looters. A special militia unit had been set up composed of soldiers and police who roamed the city in protective uniform, shooting vandals first and not stopping to ask questions later.

The bodies were dumped south of the river in Battersea Park, but they rotted untouched, since the spiders were interested in live prey.

And by all reports the spiders were mutiplying fast.

The nervousness of the Action Committee was increasing minute by minute.

Inspector Bradshaw informed the committee of what had been discovered, including a verbatim account of the meeting with Frank Kendrick.

"The stupid bastard!" General Harper commented. "If he'd spoken up before this, the whole thing would never have happened."

"Yes, I'm sure we all agree with you, General," Bradshaw nodded. "But we can't do anything about that now. What's more worrying in the short term is that it now seems we may have at least one other type of spider to deal with eventually. Alan, would you like to explain?"

Alan stood up. Dark hollows under his eyes showed lack of sleep, and he supported himself on the edge of the desk as he spoke in a quite, firm voice.

"Inspector Bradshaw is right. We're used to the hunting packs of black spiders, and the sprinkling of "giants" that run with them. But there's yet another type of spider which, for reasons I'm not sure of, has so far only revealed itself in the early attacks on Frank Kendrick's cattle. This type is large, and light brown in color—and according to Kendrick it does not eat them. Instead it poisons its victims, then abandons them. This phenomenon is completely unknown in natural history."

"I'm not a scientist, Mason," Sir Stanley Jenson interrupted, "but since this began, I've been doing considerable reading on spiders. Don't some species paralyze their prey with venom?"

"Certainly. But that's only to make it easier for them to eat the prey later. In such cases the poison also acts to aid digestion breaking down the body tissues of the prey. But I'm afraid we've got something different here. . . . And that really worries me. The existence of a markedly different species suggests there may be other, even more deadly mutations breeding down in that hellhole right now."

"A point, please," General Harper barked. "Have we any proof that they *were* any different from the other spiders? After all, you said they did run off when this farmer chap shot his gun—an interesting point, I may add. I still say if we bombed them they'd soon beat it."

Alan ignored the general's last remark.

"We *know* they were different. According to Kendrick they did no outward damage to his bull. The animal got up and wandered around for nearly a day."

"Why haven't they been seen since, then?" someone asked.

Alan had been expecting that question.

"That fact, gentlemen, is something I've no idea about. But now I mean to find out."

"How?"

"By going down to investigate the research center myself. . . ."

All was still in the woods a few miles from Dragon's Farm where the terror had started. Late autumn sunlight filtered through the trees, and dead leaves floated silently to the ground, forming a carpet of brown and gold. No insects crawled through the dry leaves, no birds sang, and no squirrels scampered up and down the treetrunks. The woods had the silence of a painting—but there was no beauty in it.

In the middle of the woods, overgrown with weeds, were the crumbled remains of a building. Charred beams in the gaping roof told of a fire years ago when the building had been white and the gardens neat. The rusty remnants of a barbed-wire fence showed where the grounds had ended, and if this was followed around, it came to a gate. Over this a notice board, the paint now peeling, hung on broken hinges. All that could be made out now were a few faded letters, *GOV .... ENT PROP .. TY*, for anyone there to read them. But no one had been in the vicinity of the ruins for years.

A carefully selected position, it was too far for the local schoolchildren to wander up to, and there were no roads nearby which might tempt a curious traveler or tourist to explore. In fact, probably the last man who had walked through these woods was Frank Kendrick, a rifle crooked in his arm, looking for rabbits. Of course, now there were no rabbits either.

But there was some movement in the otherwise silent woods. Something else covered the ground besides dead leaves. . . . Spiders. Long lines of them moved back and forth from what once had been the main building of the research center complex.

The spiders marching toward the ruins, spiders little larger than normal, carried in their front legs bits of flesh—sometimes whole creatures paralyzed by venom. The macabre procession clambered over rotting wood, through crumbling stone and plaster and splinters of glass. They headed purposefully toward a large hole in the wall of the silent ruin and carefully swung themselves down a series of stone steps into a basement that had once housed files and specimens of their own kind.

And in the darkness of the basement the food-carrying insects would lay down their loads, then turn and go out again in the never ending search for live prey. Be they large or small, as long as their victims had flesh and blood it did not matter.

And when these hunter spiders had gone, large, dark shapes—some as big as giant turtles, others as small as a man's fist—would emerge from the darkness and slide slowly across the damp surface, which was strewn with maggot-ridden rotting meat and bones.

These dark shapes, some black, some light brown, gorged themselves on the food, then returned to tend their young, newly hatched or still concealed inside the silk egg-sacs, waiting to emerge.

Time, of course, meant nothing to these creatures. They survived through cycles of birth and death. When a mother pierced the egg sac she had protected for so long, she usually died; and the young spiderlings, born with a savage greed, tasted their first flesh—that of the creature which had brought them into the world. And when the females of the new brood in turn brought their newly born into the world, they, too, would lie down and die in the ultimate sacrifice.

But not all the spiders followed this pattern. Only the hunter species succoured their young this way. The larger black types survived for years; some had even been there since the time of the fire.

When the fire had swept through the buildings so many years ago, most of the spiders had been lodged on the ground floor, in cages that stretched along the long walls of the laboratory. By a freak chance, the whole wall had collapsed together, sending the cages crashing to the floor, and breaking open the flimsy safety catches.

As the fire roared around them, the spiders had scuttled out of the building in fear. South American, Pakistani, Australian, African, as well as the newly bred British species, darted in and out of the damp undergrowth or climbed the trees in the woods.

The spiders had watched as men tried hopelessly to douse the flames. And they watched them depart and leave the building still smoldering. After a while no one had returned, leaving the ruins and the woods to the spiders.

Food was the priority and, soon all the insects round about had been devoured. *Avicularis,* the fearsome bird-eating spiders from the tropics, started to attack the woodland birds; and other spiders, such as deadly brown and black widows, joined them in stripping the carcasses. The black-backed British spiders, their gas-infected hormones running wild inside them, were soon driven by starvation to eat first other species or spiders, and then the remains of birds, squirrels, and rabbits killed by their larger cousins.

The tropical spiders returned to the ruined building, making their home in the basement, which was warmer than the open woods. And they began breeding, and crossbreeding, producing species never imagined by biologists and scientists.

Each new generation of British spider grew larger as the hormones in their bodies dictated, until they, too, crawled into the basement and cross-fertilized with their tropical cousins.

But it was the Pakistani Stegodyphus which contributed the most important link in the chain of breeding which stretched over the years. These creatures had multiplied quickly and formed communities, each group spinning huge webs through the trees to catch birds and other small animals. Any prey caught was instantly killed by the hundreds of spiders hunting on the massive web.

After all the natural wildlife in the immediate area had been wiped out, mobs of hunters roamed farther afield—and discovered larger animals to attack. Defenseless animals—cows, sheep, dogs, and pigs. And then human beings.

After years the final hybrid had emerged—a lethal deathdealer—a hunter and killer armed with a completely new poison. And they organized themselves not through intelligence, but through instinct for survival, the most basic driving force of all.

The really huge spiders could not move easily, so were in danger of starving. But they were breeding spiders and, like queen bees in a hive, they remained in the warm basement, the spiders' nursery, looked after by other, smaller types—the smallest spiders of all. The hunters also were smaller, but, as they went further afield and developed more strength, some grew larger by freak mutation—the "giants" who led the packs.

One paramount variety, the large, hairy Brown Recluse spider—brought originally from South America —had once used its venom to completely paralyze its prey, killing the victim's tissue, a sort of "freezing" process. But the venom had become affected gradually through crossbreeding, till it no longer paralyzed the victim, merely drove it mad. It was this phenomenon that Frank Kendrick had witnessed. With its loss of effectiveness the Brown Recluse had since succumbed to its black rivals.

The spiders used their strong front legs to dig under the ruins, where in winter they were warm; the dugouts were lined with thick silk, web laid upon web. Beneath the ruins a maze of interconnected lairs stretched for nearly a mile. It was a silent spawning ground of hell.

And it was this place Alan Mason intended to enter. . . .

16

Alan admitted to Bradshaw and Louise that he didn't really know what he would achieve by investigating the old research center. "But at least I'll be able to see if there's anything there. As I said, it could be that new waves and mutations of spiders are breeding in the old building, waiting for the right moment to come out. If there's nothing breeding there, we'll know that we have only to deal with the existing armies of spiders fanning outward. Then maybe that suggestion about creating a solid band of fire from the Lake District to Newcastle might not be so crazy after all."

Peter Whitley, who had been listening poised at the door of Alan's lab, disagreed with him.

"Burning a line across England won't work," he claimed, walking into the room. "I agree with you about going down to the research center. That way we'll see if they're still breeding or not. But they could still be building new lairs all over the country, even if the research center is empty. . . . I'm coming with you, by the way."

"Sorry, but I'm doing this on my own," Alan insisted.

"The hell you are!" Bradshaw exploded. "I'll be there, General Harper's men will be there, and some others, too, I hear."

"We can forget it, then," Alan said. "If a whole army of people go thundering down there, the spiders will disappear again if any are there at all, that is. No, it can't work that way. Two vans at most."

"Good," Louise said. "I'll travel with you."

"You're definitely not going!" Alan said firmly.

Louise smiled coyly. "We'll see," she murmured.

Bradshaw and Whitley left them in the lab, Bradshaw to arrange for the special vans to travel in. Alan had insisted on a security-type van, with no openings except a filtered air-vent at the top. The back and side doors could only be opened internally, and radio contact could be made from inside the van. Their protective suits had been strengthened, and two-way radios fitted inside the helmets, like spacemen's. Theoretically they were one hundred percent spiderproof.

Alan looked at Louise after the others had gone.

"I mean it, love," he said. "You're not coming on this trip."

"Sure," she smiled. "Alan, do you think we should still keep those creatures?" she said, pointing at the row of glass jars and cages lined up on the bench. She was trying hard to change the subject.

"Of course we should!" Alan snapped. "We might come up with something. But God knows what," he added, his tone dropping.

"OK, OK, I was only asking," Louise said, running her hands through her hair. She rubbed her eyes and blinked hard.

"You're tired, darling. Why not have a rest? I'm only going to look through some papers."

"I'll be all right. To tell the truth, I haven't been feeling too good all day. My bones ache and I've got a bit of a headache."

"Have you taken anything?"

"A couple of aspirin. I felt a bit better after that. Maybe I'll take some more now," she said rising from a bench stool.

Alan, who had been leaning against the wall, walked over to her and took her gently in his arms, kissing her forehead.

"I think you'll live, lovely one. You'd better, with the plans I've got in store."

She smiled, and they kissed.

He was sitting at his desk reading the results of a venom test when Louise came back.

"OK now?" he asked, without looking up.

"Yes, thanks. I've taken some more tablets," she replied. "I hope I haven't caught this new flu bug that's been going around Holland. Dutch flu, they call it, I think."

"Oh, I don't think so, darling," Alan mumbled, half listening to Louise while he concentrated on the report.

Louise sat on a stool and watched Alan leaf through the papers. She did not feel at all well, but did not want to tell Alan. He had enough trouble.

Suddenly Alan flung the papers in the air and jumped up.

"That's it!" he yelled. "That's bloody it!"

Louise was startled.

"What you just said!" he explained.

"What . . . I didn't say anything," she stuttered. "I just took two tablets, that's all."

"No! No! No! After that! About the flu!" Alan was screaming with excitement and Louise felt only bewilderment.

"Yes, I said there's a new strain called Dutch flu. Thousands of people have caught it in Holland. I said I hoped I hadn't caught it," she repeated quickly.

"Darling, darling!" Alan shouted, hugging her tightly. "You're a genius!"

He let her go and began skipping around the lab clapping his hands and laughing loudly. He thumped his fists on the bench and jumped in the air.

Louise was totally convinced he had gone mad.

"Alan, what is it?" she pleaded, but he did not reply.

Instead he rushed to a phone.

"Get me Sir Stanley Jenson. Yes, now! Sooner if possible. I don't care if it's eleven o'clock at night!" he screamed down the phone. "He's with who? Even better! The Prime Minister won't mind. Yes, of course, I want you to interrupt him. Stop wasting time and get me Sir Stanley!" he thundered and slammed the phone down.

"Will you tell me now?" Louise asked timidly.

Alan's cheeks were flushed and his eyes bright as he answered. "I think I've got the answer," he said, grinning wildly. "I think we can defeat those little bastards."

"How?"

"By . . ." the phone interrupted him. "I'll tell you in a minute," he promised, and picked up the phone.

"Sir Stanley? Yes, it's me, Mason. I think we're on to something positive now. I know you've heard that before but will you listen?" he snapped. "Can you arrange to have a sample of that flu virus flown over from Holland. The new type," he paused, listening. "I know it's an odd request, but it might just save the population of Britain. Oh, and one thing. I want a concentrated sample. The stronger and more virulent it is the better. What? I don't know how you can do it! That's your job, not mine. Use the RAF, use a Jumbo Jet, use a bleeding carrier pigeon for all I care! But get that stuff here as soon as possible!" he screamed and banged the phone down once again.

He slumped back in his seat, panting with excitement.

"Now will you tell me what all the fuss is about?" Louise asked again.

Alan nodded vigorously.

"Of course, of course. The flu bug. Spiders have no defense against virus strains. Like flu," he explained.

"Are you sure?" Louise asked, almost conditioned to the fact that the spiders were invincible.

"No, I'm not sure," his voice returning to near normal. "But we'll know as soon as we get the sample from Holland."

For the next twelve hours Alan did not sleep. He told only Bradshaw and Peter Whitley about his theory, swearing them to silence until the results of the experiment were through.

The sample arrived the next morning, brought by Harrier jet.

Alan had already prepared a cage into which he put one large spider. Deliberately starving it, he had cut up some raw meat in readiness. He took the small sample phial and extracted the flu virus in solution with a syringe, then injected the meat with it.

Opening the wire mesh lid of the cage, he dropped the meat in. The spider ignored it.

"Christ! What's happening to me!" he shouted. "Live food! We need some live food!"

Peter Whitley brought a white mouse from another lab and Alan injected it with the remainder of the serum, then almost flung it in the cage. At first the spider merely stared at the mouse scampering around. The mouse sniffed along the edge of the cage, not taking any apparent notice of the huge black insect. Suddenly the spider pounced and sank its poison fangs into the side of its neck. The mouse tried gamely to escape, but only succeeded in dragging the spider across the cage, still clinging with its fangs.

The creature put up a bit more of a struggle, but soon lay still, the poison working quickly through its system. The spider dug its jaws into the mouse again and again, tearing off chunks of meat and fur.

The grisly meal continued for nearly ten minutes. Then the spider, having satisfied its hunger, crawled to the corner of the cage, curled its legs under its heaving body and rested, its eight eyes staring coldly ahead, like those of a dead fish.

Alan behaved like a madman for the next twenty four hours. He paced around the lab, checking every ten minutes to see if the spider was still alive. He banged the top of the cage repeatedly and cursed when he saw the insect move. Peter Whitley suggested that he should grab a few hours sleep, and even managed to talk him into going upstairs, saying he would call him if anything happened.

But Alan was down two hours later, unable to close his eyes, let alone sleep.

Drinking endless cups of coffee, Alan stared fixedly at the cage, waiting for the spider to die. Fourteen hours after the first meal the spider scuttled across the cage to the remains of the mouse, and finding it dead, moved off again in search of more food.

Alan banged his desk in frustration.

"Why won't the damn thing die!"

Peter glanced at Louise, who had just come down after sleeping most of the morning. She was sniffing and her voice was thick with the effects of the flu.

"Do spiders sneeze when they've got a cold?" she asked, trying to lighten the tense atmosphere in the lab.

"No, they're meant to bloody well die!" Alan thundered.

Bradshaw arrived later, and looked in the cage. The spider still padded around, apparently as healthy as when he last saw it the night before.

"It's not working, is it?"

"We'll give it another ten hours," Peter suggested. "If it's still alive, then we're back to square one."

Alan went upstairs to his bedroom, not attempting to hide the disappointment he felt. Six hours later, after managing some sleep at last, he was back in the lab.

Peter was still watching the spider. Bradshaw was on the phone, listening to the latest reports of the spiders' movements through Britain.

Alan hurried over to the cage. Peter's face already told him that it was still alive.

"Fuck you!" he yelled. "Fuck you!"

Bradshaw looked up and shook his head.

"It seems hopeless now, doesn't it?"

Alan did not reply.

Louise, sitting in a corner with a box of tissues, said hoarsely, "Is it, Alan?"

Alan ignored her question as well. He was staring at the cage, his eyes wide.

"Look! Look! Something's happening. Its back legs! It's dragging them. It can't move them properly."

They rushed to the cage. Alan was right. The back legs were locked and the spider seemed to be having difficulty in walking. It began to move around in circles, acting confused.

"It's dying!" Peter shouted. "It's dying!"

The four of them hugged one another wildly. Alan danced around the lab, tears of relief running down his cheeks. It had worked!

"We've done it! We've beaten the bastards," he laughed. "We've won!"

Peter rushed out and came back with a bottle of whiskey and four paper cups. By the time they had toasted their success and gulped the whiskey back, the spider lay quite still. It was finally dead.

The four of them, cups in hand, stood looking at the body in silence. The enormous tension and excitement of the previous twenty-four hours had left them drained. But their strength soon returned.

"Is there any more serum?" Alan asked.

"Yes, Sir Stanley arranged for a large batch to come over. It's downstairs."

"Thank God he did *something* right!" Alan said. "You fetch it while I put these other spiders into the cage. We want to make sure that they all die."

"They will," smiled Peter. "They bloody well will!" he added, and went off to collect the serum and a couple of mice.

Alan lifted the dead body of the spider out with a pair of forceps and put it in a jar.

"I'm going to see Sir Stanley with this," he said. "Neil, can you talk to that General What's-his-name and arrange to have transporter planes at the ready?"

Bradshaw nodded and left to make arrangements.

Alan sprawled in his chair.

"We've done it, Louise," he said grinning. "Do you realize we've won, love?"

"*You've* done it, Alan," she said tenderly, her love for him at that moment mixed with enormous respect.

Peter came back with the serum and small box containing two white mice. Alan jumped up.

"Great! Now we'll finish the others off!" he said, grabbing the box and serum.

"While you're doing that I'm going to have some sleep, if you don't mind. It's been a long day, and night," Peter sighed.

"Yes, that's fine," Alan said, opening the serum packets. "Oh, and Peter," he added.

Peter turned back.

"Thanks."

"For what?"

"Just thanks," Alan said with a smile.

Peter walked out, feeling tired and excited at the same time. And proud to have been in on one of the great historical moments in science.

Alan filled two syringes with serum, and injected the struggling mice, then put them back in their box.

"And now for the other buggers," he muttered as he lifted a few jars off the bench, each containing a killer spider. He tossed them carelessly into a large cage, chuckling to himself as he did so. "You too, Charlie," he said, gingerly carrying the giant across and tipping it into the cage.

Louise laughed.

"What's so funny?" he smiled.

"You remind me of one of those mad professors in a horror movie," she told him.

"Ah, but this is the end of the horror, baby," he smirked, speaking in a mock American accent.

He was ready to drop the last spider into the cage when he looked across at Louise. She sat with her hands clasped between her knees, smiling at him.

"Could you get the serial numbers of the serum and their composition identification? We'll need it for the future."

Louise was nodding, when Bradshaw leaned around the door.

"There's a car waiting to take you to Sir Stanley. He's with the Prime Minister. I also rounded up most of the Action Committee. They're waiting with the PM now. Will you be long?"

"Just coming. I'll meet you at the car," Alan replied.

He shook the jar and tipped the last spider into the cage. Holding up the box with the mice he paused.

"You don't know how much I've looked forward to this moment," he commented, and dropped the mice in. "Bye, you little horrors. Bye Charlie."

"Right, I'm going," he said excitedly. "I'll just take this," he picked up the jar with the dead spider. "And this," he added ripping a color diagram of a spider off the wall. "And kiss my lovely lady," he leaned across and brushed his lips over Louise's forehead, "and bid you farewell."

Louise was still smiling as he hurried out. Thirty seconds later his head appeared in the doorway.

"Don't forget to do those serums."

"Off you go! I'll do them."

"Love you," he whispered, his eyes bright with excitement.

"Love you too," she smiled.

She heard him run down the corridor and went to pick up the serums. She noticed the spiders were already attacking the mice. She turned back to the cage, sickened by the sight.

She sat down to write out the numbers inscribed on the small bottles. She hummed as she worked, a lightness in her spirit she had not felt for months.

She did not hear the slight scraping of the wire-mesh cover over the cage as it moved. The cover that Alan, in his excitement, had not clipped properly into position after dropping the mice in with the spiders. The cover that Charlie was now sliding back with ease.

Louise still sat hunched over the paper she was writing on, not aware of the silent stream of spiders, thirty or more led by the giant Charlie, as it made its way across the lab floor toward her stool.

She did not see the half-starved creatures divide into two groups, one crawling quickly up the leg of the stool and the other making for the tall cabinet beside her, on which Charlie, faster than the others, already stood poised, quivering on the edge, his eyes focused on Louise.

But she felt Charlie drop on her head, felt him bite through her finger as she ran her hand through her hair. She saw the monster clinging savagely to her hand, its poison fangs sunk deep in the base of her thumb. And then she felt the pain of a dozen spiders bite through her thin nylon lab coat and into her thigh.

Screaming, she tried to stand, but the stool fell backward and she tumbled to the floor. Charlie sped quickly over her body to her face and ripped at her cheeks. She screamed Alan's name over and over until two spiders moving crazily over her, reached her jugular vein, silencing her for ever.

When two soldiers who had been on guard outside finally burst into the lab, the spiders were ripping frantically at Louise's gaping throat, blood pouring over them in rhythmic gushes. Charlie stood aside as if savoring its victory.

The soldiers staggered back, slamming the door behind them. Peter Whitley and a group of other scientists rushed along the corridor. He opened the door, looked in quickly, and closed it, turning to the waiting men, his face pasty-white.

"Just keep the door closed," he said, his voice heavy with emotion. "She's dead. The spiders can't get out. The . . . the windows are sealed. The spiders will soon be dead too." He breathed in deeply. "Louise told me earlier that she definitely had Dutch flu."

17

As Peter Whitley stood looking down at the shredded, twisted body of Louise, Alan was standing in a room at the top of a tall building in Wembley, which had become the makeshift headquarters of the Government. He was in the Prime Minister's private study, a large room which easily held the few remaining members of the Action Committee. The Prime Minister sat near the door, listening intently to what Alan was saying.

The diagram of the spider had been pinned on a wall, and Alan stood in front of it, pointing to various parts as he spoke. He had been speaking for five minutes, and every man in the room hung on his every word.

"As I was saying, the theory that spiders do not have the correct antibodies to fight flu now seems to be true," he said. "So it was just a matter of introducing a virus into their food. Once the food is eaten, the virus literally runs riot through the spiders' bodies. Around the creatures' nerve fiber, as in every living being, is a substance called myelin, which controls the nerves. This myelin is directly connected to the central nervous system, the system that in turn controls all of the body—the heart, brain, and so on.

"So if the myelin is destroyed, the central nervous system is destroyed, and the creature dies. A virus, and we know this for certain, attacks the myelin of the nerve fibers, destroying it, unless there are antibodies present to fight the virus. Human beings have these antibodies, so don't often die of influenza. But old people, whose antibodies are not so strong, *can* die from flu and pneumonia."

"Didn't Captain Cook's sailors almost wipe out a whole island by introducing the cold virus?" someone asked.

"Yes, I'd forgotten that," Alan nodded. "It's the same pattern. The natives didn't have the necessary body defenses. Just like the spiders, they had no chance."

"What about the eggs? Won't the new hatch be unaffected?"

"No," Alan said. "The virus would be passed on to any eggs inside the female and they would die before being born. Just as in human chickenpox, where the virus is passed by the mother to the unborn baby. And the very young who are already born would catch the virus as soon as they left the egg sac, because we now know most of them eat the female who spawned them."

He paused and looked around. "If I may actually say it, gentlemen, we've got the problem licked. All we have to do is gather enough serum and arrange for infected food to be dropped among the spiders."

He sat down. The men were silent for a few moments and then began clapping and shouting congratulations. Alan's hand was shaken until he thought it would fall off. They were all smiling and the Prime Minister was beaming like the proverbial Cheshire Cat.

No one took much notice of the man in a pinstriped suit, the private secretary, when he came in and whispered something in the PM's ear.

"Gentlemen, please," he said grimly, the smile gone from his face. "If you'll excuse us, I would like to speak to Mr. Mason alone."

He led the way to a door, Alan following.

"In here," the PM muttered, and the two men walked into a small anteroom lined with filing cabinets.

The Prime Minister emerged a few minutes later, visibly shaken. He closed the door softly behind him to block out the sound of Alan's sobbing.

Alan refused to be put under sedation, saying he had too much work to do. Despite the fact he had only had six hours sleep in forty-eight hours, he now worked like a man possessed. He was like a robot, doing things automatically, without any feeling.

Bradshaw and Peter Whitley tried to reason with him, but found it was like dealing with a machine. Alan refused to listen. He was obsessed with destroying the spiders. They eventually saw it was useless to talk him out of helping with its preparations for their annihilation.

"It's probably best he works with us," Bradshaw reasoned with Whitley. "It'll keep his mind off Louise."

"Are you kidding? Look at him," Peter said. "He's on a personal revenge campaign. The thought of Louise is the only thing that keeps him going."

Bradshaw shrugged, knowing Peter was right.

Massive doses of flu serum were prepared all around the world and flown into Britain. A new campaign headquarters was set up at Wembley Stadium and the army, air force, and police worked closely in coordinating plans for dropping infected food to the spider hordes.

Transporter planes and helicopters were kept on the alert twenty-four hours a day. All movements by the public around the country were stopped unless absolutely vital.

Alan worked furiously with Peter and Bradshaw to pin-point the key zones where the tainted food should be dropped.

"We've already got the pattern of their movement," he told them. "I reckon we'll have to drop the stuff every two miles along the lines starting from Dragon's Farm in Kent and radiating outward along the paths of destruction," he said, pointing to a large map marked with varicolored pins.

"What about the bait?" Alan asked. "It's got to be live."

"We've emptied nearly every cat and dog home in the country," Bradshaw replied. "Teams of vets and nurses are injecting them all now. Even the RSPCA didn't complain under the circumstances," Bradshaw smiled apologetically.

Alan gazed at him, his face immobile.

"When do we start moving in?" he asked.

"Tomorrow morning, if that's all right with you."

"Fine. I want to be on the first drop."

"Do you think that's wise?" Peter asked.

"I'm not discussing the wisdom of it," Alan said soberly. "I'm just telling you I want to be on that first trip. Can you please organize it, Neil?"

Bradshaw looked at Peter and raised his eyebrows.

"OK," he said. "You'll be on it."

"Thanks," Alan said, his lips hardly moving. "I'm only the guy that discovered the way out. Too bloody late!" he spat.

"Alan. . . ."

"Don't! I was so full of my own ego that I left that lid unclipped. You know it, I know it. Well, I'll say it!" he snarled. "I killed her! Yes, me! So bloody proud of what I'd done I couldn't wait to show off to the Prime Minister. If I'd stayed at the lab, Louise would still be alive."

He laughed, but it was a laugh that made Bradshaw and Peter shiver, a demon laugh, the laugh of a crazy man.

"Do you know?" he smiled viciously. "Do you realize that she'll go down in history? Probably the last person to be killed by the spiders. You must admit it's ironic, isn't it?"

And then he broke down.

The two men stared silently at the floor. Bradshaw, the policeman who had seen more grief than most men hear about in a lifetime; and Peter, the scientist to whom life and death were only part of a normal pattern. Both were helpless, small, in the face of Alan's despair. And they felt heavy with shared sorrow.

The huge transporter helicopter stood on the tarmac its engine running. Another dozen helicopters stretched to its right, and at the end of the runway a transporter plane stood by, its wide doors at the front fully open.

A former RAF station just outside Bedford had been taken over as the main launch point; the military had worked out that from there every spider-infested area would be within the fuel range of the helicopters. It had been decided that the plane would only be used as a back-up, not having the versatility of the 'copters.

Alan stood beside the first chopper and watched in silence as the cats and dogs were brought up. The animals, injected only twenty-four hours before, were still frisky and struggled to be free of their handlers as they were placed in a large harness fixed to the undercarriage of the helicopter, with a control cable leading inside the main cabin.

Several animals were put in each harness. The noise was almost deafening as they barked and squealed in terror, as if knowing what was coming.

Bradshaw walked across the tarmac toward Alan.

"Think that'll be enough?" he asked, nodding at the wriggling desperate animals.

"I think so. Where are we going?" Alan said tonelessly.

"Near Luton. It's the furthest north the spiders have reached," Bradshaw told him.

Alan strode toward the helicopter. Although the whole operation of preparing the serum worldwide, flying it to Britain, and collecting the animals for injection had only taken five days, to Alan it seemed a lifetime. After he had collapsed through grief and sheer exhaustion, he had been taken to a nearby emergency hospital and put under sedation. Alan had slept for thirty-six hours, but when he awoke he did not feel refreshed. His mind drove his body relentlessly and he was again the walking zombie he had been before collapsing.

He hauled himself up into the passenger cabin and sat on the hard seat by the large window, looking down on the edge of the harness. Bradshaw and a few others from the Action Team, including General Harper, joined him, and the door was closed.

The propellers swung up and whirred noisily as the pilot increased their speed. The helicopter lifted suddenly and rose quickly into the air, hauling the harness with it. Alan looked down and saw the trapped animals swing back and forth in their steel-rope cage.

He could not hear them bark and shriek above the noise of the propellers, but he saw the fear in their bulging eyes as the harness tightened around them, squeezing the animals against each other. He saw their jaws open and close as they felt the air speed by, and watched as they fought to escape, trying to clamber over each other, clawing madly in attempts to break the cords of the harness.

Alan watched horrified as one labrador, gnawing at the steel, ripped the side of its jaw, the blood spattering over the animals behind it. He looked away quickly.

He had worked with, played with, animals like these for most of his life. And as he took them to their awful death, he thought of Professor Boyd and the experiments carried out at the research center. But at least *I'm* trying to save lives, human lives, he reasoned. And with the thought, the picture of his father's body swam into his mind, immediately replaced by that of Louise. . . .

He looked back at the animals in the harness. What

had to be done, had to be done. There was no alternative.

They reached Luton in fifteen minutes. It had been
decided that the first drop would be north, and the
plan was to work backward toward Kent, through London. That way the spiders' *advance* would be halted.
Alan had agreed that was the best plan.

Working from coordinates obtained by aerial reconnaissance, the pilot slowed down and hovered over a
deserted suburban housing estate. The helicopter gently
descended above the houses.

Immediately below lay a large patch of ground covered with countless spiders. From the air it looked as if
someone had dropped soot on the pavements and a
soft wind was blowing it along. The pilot moved the
chopper nearer to the ground, looking for a clear space
to let the harness down. There were thirty feet of cord
between the harness and the undercarriage. He could
not move among the houses. General Harper saw the
difficulty, and grunted.

"Why the hell haven't we got a hundred-foot winch
on the damned thing?" he snapped at a major beside
him.

The man shrugged.

"Well, make sure the others have one!" he said angrily. "This is crazy!"

For the first time in five days Alan smiled. Bureau-
cracy runs true to form, he thought.

The pilot eventually spotted a large traffic circle
swarming with the insects and lowered the 'copter over
it. Everyone was at the windows as the harness
touched the ground, and then flattened as it was lowered another few feet.

The pilot punched the release button and the cord
snaked down on top of the harness, opening it to release the animals.

The dogs bounded out, tails wagging and barking

excitedly. For a few minutes they ran hither and thither. But they soon stopped running and began fighting for their lives, as the spiders swamped the doomed animals.

It was a scene of merciless carnage. The animals had no chance as they bit and scratched for survival. Dogs hurled themselves into the air in an attempt to flee the hordes and attacking insects. But soon the animals lay exhausted and bleeding, covered with mounds of black, writhing, death.

No one spoke as the helicopter swung up and headed back toward Bedford. There was no laughter, no cheering, no back-slapping. The grisly sight had shocked them too much. But it was a sight they would get used to over the next two days as the operation was repeated scores of times in deserted streets and parks. . . .

18

"I've quite decided. It's no use trying to change my mind," Alan said firmly, glaring at Inspector Bradshaw and General Harper. "I'm going into that building. I've got to see where it all started, perhaps find out how."

"I'm not arguing with you about that," Harper said. "It's just this crazy notion of you going it alone. You don't know what's in that place. I'm saying you should take a few of my men with you."

"He's right, Alan," Bradshaw agreed. "As a matter of fact I've got the authority to arrest you to prevent you from making this trip on your own. And I'll do it," he said.

Alan sighed.

"OK, OK," he nodded. "But, as I said before, I don't want a battalion of men marching in there. No more than a dozen. Right?"

"Right," the general snapped. "I'll pick the men myself."

"You'll only need eleven. I'm going as well," Bradshaw told him.

"That's up to you," Harper shrugged. "My men'll be ready in one hour."

It was the morning after the first drop. According to early reports, the spiders had already begun to die around the Luton area, and helicopters were operating a shuttle service between Bedford and the various dumping points. The biggest fear was that there might be a shortage of dogs and cats to infect and feed the spiders. But the Prime Minister had signed a special order authorizing the police and militia to possess household pets if necessary. As yet they had not been needed—luckily, thought Alan when he heard of the order.

The two vans Alan had asked for were ready. He and Bradshaw climbed into the first one, along with five of the soldiers. Another six men from the militia squad followed in the second van.

As General Harper watched the vans drive away through London, he turned to the major at his side.

"Give them half an hour and send the guns after them. The big ones. I've got a hunch they'll be needed."

Alan shifted uncomfortably inside his protective suit. The van moved fast through the deserted city and was soon passing Blackheath. Through the small windows he could see a few of the enemy still straggling across the heath, looking for food which was not there.

"They'll soon have plenty to eat," Bradshaw chuckled, his voice tinny through the radio receiver inside Alan's helmet.

Only the inspector and Alan could communicate with each other this way. There had not been time to rig all the suits with radios, but Alan had briefed the men before the start of the mission.

"Remember," he had said, "we're only going in to see what's there. If you come across trouble, get out quick. These bastards will be vicious."

The men got the message. No one wanted to be a dead hero.

Harper had made a good choice. The men, all marine commandos, were tough and experienced. Alan realized the general had been right in insisting they join him. There was little talk. The soldiers sat with their helmets on their knees, rocking backward and forward as the van raced toward Kent.

At last they were drawing up outside Dragon's Farm. In the hard winter frost it looked every bit as peaceful as the first time old Dan Mason had seen it.

"Where to now, sir?" the driver asked.

"There used to be a small road leading through those woods to the research center," Bradshaw pointed. "It's probably completely overgrown by now, but it should take us some of the way."

He pulled out an ordinance survey map of the area.

"I've had the old road marked on this. Let's see what we can find," he said, handing the map to the driver's assistant.

They drove around the back of the farmhouse and over a rough country lane for about a mile. Cutting to the left, the driver followed what had obviously once been a narrow tarmac road. But now, as Bradshaw predicted, it was pitted and overgrown with weeds.

As the van bumped its way into the woods, the men began to put on their helmets.

"Can you hear me?" Bradshaw asked, testing his radio device.

"Loud and clear," Alan replied.

Soon it was impossible for even the independent suspension of the van to cope with the rough conditions. The following van slowed to a halt behind the first. The soldiers jumped down and waited for orders.

The inspector gestured to his right, and the eleven soldiers, with Alan and Bradshaw leading, filed into the woods, leaving the drivers and their companions sitting safe inside the sealed cabins.

Not a breeze stirred the trees, and everything was still as the men crunched over dead leaves. Suddenly Alan stopped, pointing to the ground. A group of small spiders scattered.

"Look over there," he told Bradshaw, waving toward the edge of a small clearing.

A line of large hunter spiders moved rapidly through the undergrowth, each one carrying prey. They took no notice of the men, but, driven by instinct, headed toward the ruined buildings beyond.

Moving in a wide arc, the men approached the central research building from the side, and stood in a group watching the seemingly endless ribbon of spiders march in, through a large hole at the base of a wall. Another file of hunter spiders flowed out, their loads deposited.

So they *were* still breeding here. Alan knew his fears were justified.

"Has everything been checked?" he asked abruptly.

He saw Bradshaw nod.

Each soldier gripped a flamethrower in one hand, the cylinder strapped to his back, and a powerful torch in the other hand. From their belts hung submachine guns and ice picks—the latter in case they had to break through walls of rubble.

Alan, too, had a double cylinder pack on his back, but his contained a nerve gas hopefully capable of stunning or even killing spiders. He had a pick, but no gun, attached to his belt.

"Get two men to burn up the columns of spiders going in and out," Alan told Bradshaw. "That way, the rest of us can get in without interference."

Bradshaw made the necessary signals and two soldiers split off, flamethrowers at the ready, and slowly approached the building. Just before reaching the lines of insects, they released the jets of flame, aiming directly at the creatures. The dead leaves burst into flame, and the spiders scattered. A scorched blackness appeared under the flame, which the oncoming spiders tried to move around, blind instinct forcing them on. But the men, now standing on the burned ground, had no difficulty in keeping them at bay. Back to back, they sprayed instant death on the two columns advancing and retreating.

Alan led the rest of the men toward the ruins. The stark, crumbling walls and the gaping black windows gave no indication of what lay inside. No spiders crawled from the windows or over the walls; no webs covered the rotting, charred frames.

It was *too* quiet, thought Alan as he approached a gap in the wall, once a doorway. He stepped over the threshold and was immediately plunged into darkness. He tried to move forward but found himself stuck, his arms and legs caught on a huge web, spun across the inside of the door.

As he struggled to free himself, he realized why the building looked so dark from the outside. Every door and window was covered with a solid curtain of sticky web extending all around inside the ruins. It was a giant cocoon, and Alan understood why the hunter spiders only used one entrance. It was the only one left open.

Bradshaw's voice crackled through the radio.

"Don't move! We'll burn the web from the top."

Unable to turn, Alan felt the heat of the flame-thrower above him as the thick web disintegrated. With strands of web clinging to him, he cautiously moved into the room that had known no human footstep for over forty years. He aimed his flashlight on the floor, its bright beam cutting sharply through the darkness.

Alan recoiled with disgust. Hundreds of bones lay there—the remains of the countless animals devoured for food. Skulls of all shapes and sizes grinned grotesquely up at him. He did not examine them too closely, frightened of what he might find. He swung the flashlight around the room, picking out more bones and fragments of rotting skin and fur.

But not a single spider.

He crossed the room.

"I'm going through to the center of the building," he spoke into his microphone.

"We're right behind you," Bradshaw said immediately. "I'd get that gas ready, if I were you."

"Will do," Alan said, and unhitched the long nozzle from his belt.

He crunched across the bones and through another doorway, and found himself in the main reception area. Suddenly he saw them. Small hunter spiders streamed from his right, heading for the hole in the external wall, through which Alan could see the reflected glow from the flamethrowers outside.

He shone his flashlight in the direction from which the spiders were coming.

He breathed in sharply as he saw an open doorway with steps leading down to the basement. The spiders were literally pouring out of it, seemingly from the very earth itself.

"In the basement," he said flatly. "That's where they are. I'm going down."

"Be careful, for God's sake, man!" Bradshaw's voice came through urgently.

Standing at the top of the steps, Alan shone his flashlight down. Some men came up behind him and followed his example, lighting up the whole expanse of cellar floor. It was covered with rotting carnage. Then Bradshaw grabbed Alan's arm as the torch picked out what seemed to be a group of large, immobile bodies.

But they were almost transparent, like ghosts.

"Moulted skins," Alan explained briefly. "It means the giant spiders are around here somewhere."

As they shone their flashes around the whole room, more bones reflected in the light. But still there was no sign of any really large spiders—only the small hunters.

Alan started to descend the steps, careful not to slip on the slimy pieces of old, green meat. He crunched the bodies of hunter spiders underfoot. The vicious insects began to crawl over the mens' suits, looking for any space into which they could sink their jaws. Then hunter spiders started to rain from the ceiling, covering their visors.

Alan wiped them away, feeling grim satisfaction when he saw them bite uselessly on the tough material. Followed by the others in single file, he reached the foot of the stairs and moved to the center of the room, shining his flashlight around.

"Look!" he gestured. "Around the walls! Tunnels!" A series of low passages, about three feet high and six across, radiated out from the base of the wall all around the room. Newly spun webs of thick silk stretched across each opening.

With a sudden jab of panic, Alan realized what they were.

"Get back!" he motioned. "We've got to get out! These tunnels are where—"

He was interrupted by Bradshaw.

"Move, man. Move!" the inspector yelled.

A soldier, one of the last in the row, had slipped on the stairs and came crashing down toward Alan. The man landed in a crumpled heap on the floor, tried to stand, then pointed at his leg. It was broken. Hundreds of hunter spiders clambered over him, almost hiding him from view.

Two other soldiers went to help him up, but not Alan. He was staring, horrified, as dozens of pairs of thick, massive legs began to appear from the holes all around the room. These were by far the biggest spiders they had seen—absolute monsters.

He grabbed Bradshaw's arm and pointed, too stunned to speak. Slowly the spiders emerged from every hole. The men were surrounded.

Terrified, they watched the huge beasts come silently out of the tunnels toward them. Each monster was five feet wide and stood nearly three feet high. Their bristle-covered black bodies were nearly six feet long, and because of their bulk the creatures almost slid along, their bellies only a few inches from the ground.

Bradshaw was the first to act. A spurt of flame shot from his flamethrower at one of those nearest him. The hellish creature halted for a few seconds, then began to advance again. Bradshaw aimed the flame higher, directly at its head, and this time the monster dropped to the ground, curling its legs beneath it. But, to the inspector's horror, another spider began to emerge from the same tunnel. By the light of his torch he could see another behind. . . .

The men gathered in a tight circle, spitting flame outward at the advancing monsters. It seemed hopeless. As soon as one was killed, another took its place. Alan sprayed his nerve gas over them and two collapsed in front of him. But he knew it was only a matter of time before both nerve gas and flame ran out.

"The stairs!" he shouted. "Make for the stairs!"

Bradshaw waved an arm at the men who moved as one toward the steps.

Alan felt the sweat running over his body as the heat in the basement increased. He thought he was going to faint, but pulled himself together, pushing against Bradshaw, forcing his way toward the stairs.

The men moved around the thrashing body of the injured soldier, and Alan watched panicstricken as one of the spiders reached the man and raised its enormous, pincer-like, biting jaws. It lowered its head and the jaws opened wide, then snapped shut at the top of his shoulder. The whole arm came away—blood spurting from the ragged hole in the soldier's suit.

One of the leading soldiers turned and aimed his flamethrower at the killer, but stood helpless as the flame spluttered and died. He struggled to pull his machine gun up, but the spider reached him first and sliced through his leg. The man fell, and the other spiders began to rip him open.

The soldiers, dropping the flamethrowers and seizing

their submachine guns, began to spray bullets wildly
around the basement. But the spiders kept coming, and
coming. Alan saw one man stumble and fall forward,
his gun arcing wildly. He did not have time to
straighten up before another spider caught his head in
its jaws and sliced cleanly through the neck.

Bradshaw was already on the stairs, frantically beck-
oning to Alan and the remaining soldiers. Alan began
to move toward the steps, but the dead carcasses of
spiders and the bleeding bodies of the soldiers, now
carpeted with smaller, hunting spiders, slowed his
progress.

He was only a few feet from Bradshaw when another monster sidled in front of him. He aimed the gas
nozzle, but the beast seized it in its biting jaws,
crumpling the steel tube like paper.

Alan could see the huge eyes gazing hatefully at him
as the spider lumbered forward. Dropping the now useless nozzle, he pulled his ice pick free and brought it
down heavily on top of the attacker's body. It glanced
off harmlessly.

The monster now raised its head to bite Alan
through the midriff. With tears of fear running down
his cheeks, Alan lifted the ice pick again and aimed
directly for one of the two large center eyes. He felt
the axe sink through the soft jellylike substance and
watched the spider suddenly collapse, its brain pierced.
Darting around it to the stairs he bounded up them,
slipping once, and finished his desperate escape on his
hands and knees.

Bradshaw waited at the top with four soldiers, the
only survivors of the battle. The six men stumbled ex-
haustedly through the charred entrance and out to the
waiting vans. A quick journey brought them back to
the old farmhouse.

There they discovered General Harper and a dozen
large artillery trucks trailing guns.

Alan pulled his helmet off.

"Blow it up!" he gasped. "Destroy it completely! God knows how many of them there are! They've tunneled all through the earth. You'll have to blow up everything for about two miles all around!" he panted.

The general did not hesitate and immediately sent the guns in. For an hour Alan sat in the van, listening to the explosions and watching the thick blanket of smoke rise over the woods. If there were any left alive, he thought, they would be killed by the infected prey soon to be dropped around the woods.

It was finally over, he told himself, his body leaden with exhaustion.

Alan rode back to London with the general and Bradshaw.

"They've cleared London now," Harper told them. "You can go and collect your things from the lab if you feel up to it, Alan."

Alan knew he would have to return to the lab sometime. It might as well be today, he thought. He could not feel any emotion anyway. He was numb after the horrific fight in the basement.

He nodded. "Take me there now," he said quietly.

The army vehicle pulled up outside the lab. As Alan walked away, the general leaned out.

"Congratulations, Alan," he called after him. "We've done it. We've won the war."

Alan raised his hand but did not turn around. He made his way slowly up the stairs to the bedroom he had shared with Louise.

And as he stood in the bedroom gazing at Louise's clothes scattered over the bed, tears formed in his eyes as he tried to remember a saying he had heard years ago.

Something about winning a battle, but losing a war. . . .

POSTSCRIPT

Three days after the research center was blown up, the killer spiders stopped their advance. Many of the creatures crawled out into the streets and roads to die. Squads of soldiers, police and public volunteers scoured London and the surrounding countryside for traces of living spiders.

There were none.

London again returned to normal. Time passed. The horrors of the spiders were gradually forgotten.

Nature slowly reasserted herself and the countryside was filled again with the song of birds and the scurrying of wildlife. No spiders appeared except normal garden varieties. After a year the special teams set up to keep watch for killer spiders were disbanded.

But Alan Mason, now a professor, spent many sleepless nights wondering if just one had escaped . . . if in one of the tens of thousands of gardens in Britain, the killer spiders were quietly breeding once more. . . .